SECURITY BREACH

*Rogue Security and Investigation Series
Book One*

By Evan Grace

SECURITY BREACH

Copyright © 2018 by Evan Grace.
All rights reserved.
First Print Edition: March 2018

Crave Publishing, LLC
Kailua, HI 96734
http://www.cravepublishing.net/

Formatting: Crave Publishing, LLC

ISBN-13: 978-1-64034-329-0
ISBN-10: 1-64034-329-6

No part of this book may be reproduced, scanned, or distributed in any printed or electronic form without permission. Please do not participate in or encourage piracy of copyrighted materials in violation of the author's rights. Thank you for respecting the hard work of this author.

This is a work of fiction. Names, characters, places, and incidents either are the product of the author's imagination or are used fictitiously, and any resemblance to locales, events, business establishments, or actual persons—living or dead—is entirely coincidental.

DEDICATION

To Jim, just because I love you.

Chapter One

Reece

I pull into the underground parking garage of my new job, Rogue Security and Investigation. After climbing out of my car—my pride and joy, a red 1967 Shelby GT500—I make my way to the elevator and ride it up to the top floor.

The place is seriously incredible. It's all modern: glass, black, and chrome. There's a woodsy scent in the air. A beautiful blonde sits behind the desk just outside the elevators. "Good morning," she says. "You must be Mr. Meyers. Mr. Mackenzie said you'd be joining us today." She holds out a couple of what look like credit cards to me. "Here are your keycards. The black one will get you on the elevator in the future—they kept them unlocked when they saw you coming on the monitors. The silver card will get you through any door in the back."

I take the cards from her. "Thanks."

"Mr. Mackenzie knows you're here and said to go on back to his office. It's down the first hall, last door on the right. Welcome to Rogue Security and Investigation."

"Thank you, um…"

"My name is Carrie. My husband, Egan, is one of the computer specialists here."

I stick my hand out and she shakes it. That's when I see she's pregnant. "Nice meeting you, Carrie, and congratulations."

She gives me a bright smile before I use my card to get into the back. The first thing I notice is that it's real quiet here. I was expecting it to be bustling, but instead it seems laid-back. I turn to the right and see closed office doors with nameplates on them. I find Jack's and give a knock.

"Come in," I hear, muffled from inside.

When I open the door, I find Jack standing behind his desk. Jack Mackenzie is a buddy of mine from my Army days—we were both Special Forces and did two tours together before he was honorably discharged for taking a bullet to the hip, shattering it and leaving him to get it replaced at thirty-eight years old. That was three years ago.

When I left the Army a year ago, I'd been aimless while I tried to readjust to civilian life. Luckily, I had a nice little nest egg saved while I figured out what the fuck I wanted to do with my life. My parents, being the sweet people they are, let me stay with them temporarily in my hometown of DeWitt, Illinois. Was I thrilled to be living with my parents at thirty-three? No, but it was only temporary, so I could deal.

Six months ago, Jack contacted me, and I drove up to Chicago to meet him for dinner and to discuss his business. At first, I had assumed I'd be a glorified security guard—and if that was the case, I wasn't going to take the job—but then he showed me all the information about his company. In three years, he'd taken it from three employees to a group of fifteen. There are two computer experts, three bounty hunters, and ten private investigators. He also uses off-duty law enforcement officers when needed.

I went home and thought about it, then drove back out a month later to sign my contract. I'm just now starting because I had to get licensed as a private investigator. I found a house and moved to Oak Park, a suburb of Chicago. I would've loved to live in the city, but for what I would pay for an apartment I could easily buy a house, so that's what I did.

Now that I can size him up face to face again, I see my former Army buddy still looks great. His hair is more silver than blond since he was discharged, and the crow's feet around his brown eyes are a little more pronounced. He comes around to greet me with a back slap and a hug. "Glad you're finally here, brother."

"Thanks, man. I'm happy as hell to be here and ready to get started."

"Come have a seat." I sit in the chair next to him, turning it until we're facing each other. "Did you get all unpacked?"

Jack and some of the guys helped me unload the moving truck and set up my furniture. "Yeah, I did. Thanks again for bringing the guys to help. I appreciate it."

"Not a problem. We were happy to help. Erik's going to take you with him today and just kind of show you around. My plan is to have my daughter get your paperwork all together to fill out."

"*Daughter?* I didn't know you had any kids. Especially one that's old enough to work here."

He laughs. "Yeah, I was twenty when her mom got pregnant. We were young and it didn't last, so it's not something I like to talk about." A solemn expression crosses his face, but then he shakes his head. "But Delilah moved here two years ago, and it's been great. And I'm going to be a grandpa in about four months, actually."

"Congrats, man. Does that mean we should expect to see you in big old man cardigans and bifocals?"

He laughs and gives me a shove. "Fuck you, asshole. Let's go. I'll introduce you to Erik."

Erik is a tall Viking-looking motherfucker. I'm a big guy, but he makes me feel like a shrimp. His blond hair is shaved close to the scalp, just like my own dark brown hair. I've never seen eyes more intense than this guy's piercing ice blue ones. He reaches his hand out. "I'm Erik. Nice meeting you."

"Reece. Nice meeting you too."

"Come on, I'll take you around." Side by side, we make our way toward the elevator and head down to the parking garage. He spots my car and freezes. "Is that a Shelby?"

I grin. "Yep, that's my baby. You wanna take a look at it?" He's like a kid at Christmas; he actually *runs* toward it. As he trails his hand lovingly over the red paint, he walks around the car slowly. I unlock the door and pop the hood. "Take a look at the engine. My dad and I rebuilt it."

"If you're not doing anything tonight after dinner, you ought to come by my place. I've got a 1970 Chevy Impala."

"I'm still unpacking, but fuck yeah, I want to see it. Let's do it soon."

I lock up my baby and we move across the garage to a souped-up black Explorer. We drive around, and he shows me different areas and the businesses we do the security for. During the ride, Erik tells me he's a Marine who served two tours before he got out.

"Most of the guys are former military, except for Carrie's husband," he says. "He used to do freelance work for the government. The guy is fucking smart. I figure if their kid looks like her with his brains, he or she will rule the world."

We stop at Portillo's for lunch. After picking up our food, we grab a table and conversation is stalled while we eat. This is the best Italian beef I've ever had, and if I were alone, I'd probably moan around each bite.

"So, is Egan the only one married?" I ask after wiping my mouth and tossing my napkin down.

"No, Scott and Will are both married, but the rest of us are single. What about you?"

I shake my head. "No, I'm not married, and very single."

"Good. We all tend to go out a lot together…have card games and what have you. You'll notice we're a close-knit group. It's just like the military: we're brothers."

"That's why I came to work here. That's one thing I miss about my Army days...the brotherhood."

"I hear you. I met Jack through a mutual friend and we got to talking. He asked me about my future, and to be honest, I had *no* fucking idea what I wanted to do. Him offering me the job came at the right time, because I was just sitting around with my thumb up my ass—unsure about everything and missing the hell out of my brothers. I'm now the head of investigation and surveillance, and I fucking love it."

We take off and head back to the office. I use my keycard to get us on the elevator and upstairs. He then takes me around to meet some of the guys.

Egan is not what I pictured at all. I assumed that, him being the computer expert and all, he'd be nerdish, not built like a brick shit house. He's certainly not as big as Erik, but he's bulky.

Marcus is ex-Navy and African-American: tall, with compact muscles, light-brown skin, and hazel eyes. He does a lot of the bounty hunting and is covered in a lot of badass ink. Dalton is the next guy I meet. He's tall, on the leaner side, sports a beard, and doesn't look threatening at all, but he's some sort of martial arts expert and runs surveillance with Erik.

Most of the other guys I met when they helped me move my furniture. Erik, Marcus, Dalton, and Egan had been working at the time, so they hadn't been there.

Erik leads me into the conference room and tells me to have a seat. "I'll go grab Del for you, so she can get you started on the paperwork. And just to warn you: there's a ton of it."

I reach out to shake his hand. "Thanks for showing me around today."

"You bet. We'll talk later."

On a cart by the door are bottles of water. I grab one, open it, and slug down half of it before I even sit down. I hear footsteps approach and assume it must be Jack's daughter.

The door swings open. I take one look at her, and all I can say is, "It's you."

Chapter Two

Delilah

"Is your dad still trying to convince you to tell him who Junior's dad is?"

I turn away from the mirror to look at my best friend, Brandon. We met in kindergarten and became tight right away. He's been my rock through each bad relationship my mom has been in, and when I'd be stressed about my dad when he was overseas fighting. Then when he came out to me, I was his rock when he told his family.

When I moved here to be close to my dad, Brandon didn't hesitate to come with me. And when four-and-a-half months ago I realized I'd missed two periods and was pregnant from my one and only one-night stand, he was there, and has been ever since. His green eyes gaze at me with a love that always warms me. His light-brown hair is coiffed perfectly, and he's dressed in a fitted suit that shows off his lean frame. Black eyeglasses finish off the outfit and give him the hot, nerdy look.

"No, thank God. I don't see what the point is. I never got his last name and he was here on business." It had been the best night of my life, but when I woke the next morning, he was gone. No note…nothing.

"Well, I can't wait to meet my nephew. He's going to be the best-dressed baby out there." I smile and walk into his waiting arms. "You know I'll always be there for you. Even as your coach when you're pushing him out." He makes a disgusted face that makes me laugh.

"I know you will—that's why this baby's middle name is going to be Brandon." He tears up the way he always does when I tell him that. He's also going to be my son's "fairy godfather," or at least that's what he's calling himself.

When my dad first met him, he didn't know what to make of him. Brandon is very flouncy and charismatic, and he loves laying it on thick sometimes. Now…well, now my dad, Mr. Big Bad Former Special Forces, loves him. I think it's because my dad knows that Brandon keeps an eye on me. Hell, we keep an eye on each other.

"Does this look okay?" I signal to the form-fitting dress I'm wearing. My belly has popped out a lot in the last couple of weeks, but I'm not quite ready to start buying maternity clothes yet. The dress is emerald green with capped sleeves and a v-neck that shows off my ever-growing cleavage. My breasts have always been on the smaller side, but now they're full. The dress hits me right above my knees.

"You look gorg. That color has always looked so great on you. Wear your hair up in a messy knot. Show off that rack." He kisses my cheek and then leaves to get to his internship at the advertising agency where he hopes to work when he graduates.

I finish doing my hair and then slip a pair of heels on before grabbing my purse and heading out the door. It's nice being close to the L train and not having far to walk. Luckily when I step on, there's a seat that's open. It normally takes about fifteen minutes to get to my stop, and while I wait, I pull out my phone, opening my Kindle app.

Reading romance is about the only romance for me these days. I've dated a little bit, but it never amounts to anything more than friendship. Plus, when they find out I'm pregnant, I pretty much become undesirable, like pregnancy is a disease or something.

The L approaches my stop and I stand up, holding on to the back of my seat. As soon as the doors open, I'm the first one out. I make my way down the stairs and to the street.

When I graduated from my online two-year college program with a degree in office management, my mom told me I was wasting my time and that it was a stupid choice. "You're not smart enough to manage an office," she said. Obviously, she enjoys making me feel like an idiot.

That's why I moved to be by my dad, my biggest cheerleader. As soon as I graduated, he hired me to run his office. My dad is the best at what he does, but when I started, his office was a mess. It took me over a month to get everything cleaned up and organized.

I spent so many years separated from my dad, and now that we work together, I get to see him all the time. He knows what I dealt with living with my mom, and I know a part of him still feels guilty, but he was serving our country and I can't be mad about that. When he got shot, I lost my shit. Especially since he was being treated overseas and I didn't get to see him until he was finally back stateside.

When I found out I was pregnant, my mom screamed at me over the phone for two hours about how I was screwing my life up and I should abort it. Dad was upset, but got over it really quick when my morning, noon, and night sickness started freaking Brandon out and he called him.

For a month after my mom found out, she called me at least once a week asking if I'd had the abortion yet, and I'd just hang up on her. Finally, my dad got tired of seeing me so upset and told my mom that if she couldn't be happy for me, or at least fake it, she didn't need to bother calling.

That was two months ago, and I haven't heard from her since. It hurts, but that's what she loves doing—hurting me. Never physically, but she's been the queen of emotional and mental pain for most of my life.

I enter the building and use my keycard to get on the elevator.

"Hey girlie, how are you feeling?" Carrie greets me. She's two months further along than I am, and she and her husband are possibly the cutest couple I've seen.

"I'm good," I tell her. "I actually feel great."

"That dress *looks* so great on you. Your little belly is just the cutest."

I smile and rub a hand over my tummy. "Thanks. I'm just not ready for a maternity wardrobe yet."

"This little man likes to stretch his legs and poke me in the ribs."

Since we're both having boys, we've already decided they're going to be best friends. I promise her we'll have lunch later this week, then head toward the back and step inside my office. I've got HR stuff to do with a new employee today who also happens to be a friend of my dad's. He's currently out with Erik, the office flirt. He's harmless, and I swear he only hits on me because it pisses my dad off.

Time to buckle down and get some work done before it's time to do my HR gig.

Most of my morning is spent paying bills and setting up appointments for the guys. I love that part of my job is bossing around huge ex-military men. They listen, that's for sure, and do what I say. Of course, it's probably because they're scared of my dad.

After stepping out for a quick sandwich that I eat on my way back to the office, I'm ready to meet the new guy. I grab the stack of papers and head down the hall to the conference room.

I give a knock, then open the door. He turns toward me, and I'm frozen in shock. "It's you," his deep voice rumbles.

Placing a protective hand over my belly, I don't miss when his gaze slides down my body, stopping at my bump. He stands up and moves toward me.

SECURITY BREACH

God, I forgot how big he is—so much taller than my five-foot-three frame. He rubs a hand over his head as he stands right in front of me.

I've yet to say anything, because what do I say to the man who gave me the best sex in my life, only for me to wake up and find him gone, leaving me with the greatest gift I've ever received? My mind immediately goes to that night six months ago.

Chapter Three

Delilah

Six Months Ago

It's my twenty-first birthday, and I'm on my way to a bar called The Road Trip to have drinks with some friends. I'm not much of a partier, but Brandon said if I didn't go out drinking on my twenty-first, then I'd never be allowed to step into any bars or clubs ever again. Of course he's lying, but it's not surprising that he'd use any tactic to make me come out. Hello…dramatic, much?

Brandon picked out my outfit for tonight. Since it's cold out but unseasonably warm for Chicago in December, I'm wearing black leggings and black riding boots that come up to just below my knee. Up top, I'm wearing a form-fitting, white v-neck t-shirt and a thin, lavender duster. Silver necklaces hang down the front, and silver bangles jingle from my wrists as we walk up the sidewalk to the bar.

I left my dark blonde locks in their natural

state—slightly wavy. My makeup is a little heavier than I'd planned, but if I hadn't done it, Brandon would've tied me to a chair and tried to slather a full mask on my face.

My friends tried to convince me to go to a nightclub, but I hate them. It's always loud and guys hit on us constantly, then it begins to not be any fun. I just want to drink some beer and eat some good food.

We step inside and find our friends all sitting around a large table. Hugs are exchanged, and Brandon and I take our seats across from each other.

Soon the beers have been flowing for a while, and I've had the best spicy shrimp tacos. Now we're playing darts, which I suck at. Brandon left an hour ago to meet his boyfriend, Jose, for dinner. They should be back in an hour or so. Kelsey and Emily are flirting with the group of guys who conveniently took the table right by the dart board, so they could watch us.

They tried to buy me shots, but I declined. I may be only twenty-one, but I'm not an idiot—I don't mix my alcoholic beverages, and I don't take drinks from people I don't know. I grab my purse, slip out into the main bar, and find an empty stool. The bartender stops in front of me. "What can I getcha?"

"I'll take a Summer Shandy draft, please." I pull out my phone and see a text from Brandon.

Brandon: We'll be there in about an hour. Doing okay?

Delilah: Okay, sounds good. Say hi to Jose for

me. I just ordered a beer so I'm doing fine.

Brandon: Jose says hi, and we'll see you in a bit.

The bartender sticks my beer in front of me. "That'll be four-fifty." I grab my wallet to pay the bartender, but a deep voice speaks up beside me.

"Put it on my tab." I turn to my right, and the most beautiful man I've ever seen is sitting beside me. His dark hair is shaved close to the scalp, and his eyes are a dark, mossy green. He glances at me with a warm smile. "I hope you don't mind me doing that."

"Um…not at all. Thank you. I'm Lilah, by the way." I don't know why I don't give him my full name. His woodsy scent wraps around me as I reach my hand out to shake his.

His large hand feels rough, but strong, and it fills me with a strange but welcome tingly feeling. "Reece." He turns on his stool so he faces me, and I do the same.

"Do you live here?" I ask before taking a sip of my beer.

He shakes his head. "Not yet. I was just here to talk to a buddy of mine about a job. What about you?"

"Yeah, I've lived here for two years now and love it. I live with my best friend and he's *crazy*. He actually ditched me to have dinner with his boyfriend, but I can't blame him for that. A couple of our friends are by the dart boards, but guys were starting to circle, and they were eating it up. I had to get out of there."

He eyes me suspiciously. "You don't like male attention?"

"It's not that I don't like it, but when I go out with my friends, I want to be with my *friends*, not to be some random girl that they're hoping to make a play for. It seems that if you don't return their affection, then they just move on to the next one, and that's just not okay with me."

Reece nods his head. "I can respect that. A lot of women eat that shit up, but you don't?"

"Not really. If I'm interested, then I'll let you know. What about you? You're obviously a good-looking guy. I'm sure the women in this place have been circling like vultures."

His laugh is a deep, rich sound that causes my heart to race a little bit. "They might've, but I only stopped in here because the bar at my hotel is closed for renovations, plus they told me this place had the best nachos."

As if he knew Reece was talking about it, the bartender sets a ginormous plate of nachos in front of him. "I'm gonna need your help eating these. I wasn't expecting such a huge platter."

I've never been shy around food, so I grab a chip loaded with seasoned shredded chicken, beans, lettuce, tomato, guacamole, salsa, and sour cream. I'm not embarrassed at all when I take a bite and moan. I find Reece staring at me; the look in his eyes makes my nipples hard.

"I love to see a woman who likes to eat."

"Oh yeah, I love to cook, and even more I love to eat. When I was younger, my mom used to get on me, worried that I'd get fat, but I'm really active, so obviously she had nothing to worry about." I pop the rest of my nacho in my mouth and finish off my beer.

Reece signals for the bartender and orders himself and me another beer. "I'm buying this round," I tell him, but he waves me off.

"If I let you buy, my mom would whoop my ass if she found out."

"Are you sure? That's not why I'm still sitting here."

He gives me a smile before handing me my glass. "I'm sure, and I'm aware of that because you didn't even notice me sitting here when *you* sat down."

"How do you know that?"

"I'm very observant." We both dig in with gusto, and before long, the entire plate of nachos is gone.

I've always been outgoing and have had no problem talking to people I don't know, and with Reece, it's like we've known each other forever. While we drink, he tells me that he's got a younger sister, and they all live back in his tiny little hometown in central Illinois. I share a little bit about my mom and the revolving men in and out of our lives.

"We're not very close now. She's just very critical of everything I do. I'm convinced she thinks I ruined her life. She was only nineteen when she had me, and I used to hear all the time about the stuff she didn't get to do because she was a mom." I lower my head because sometimes I have verbal diarrhea. "Sorry to be a downer."

His fingertips touch my chin and lift it, and I realize how close he is to me. I can see the gold flecks in his eyes. "Don't apologize. I've enjoyed talking to you."

I've never been forward with men before, but for some reason I'm not ready for my time to be over with him just yet. "I don't know if you have to get back to your hotel now or not, but there's this great diner about two blocks away that serves the best apple pie with a heaping scoop of homemade vanilla ice cream on top."

He doesn't even seem to think about it—Reece just signals for the bartender to close out his tab, signs the receipt, sticks his card back in his wallet, and stands up. I follow suit, and that's when I realize how *big* he is compared to me. His shirt molds to defined muscles and shows off a slim waist. Reece's jeans fit him like a second skin and highlight muscled legs. And don't think I don't notice the huge bulge in his pants...*great*. Now I'm horny.

"I'm going to tell my friends I'm leaving," I say.

"Sure, I'll be waiting right here," he says with a smile that makes my knees weak.

With quick steps, I head toward the dart boards and spot Kelsey and Emily. "Hey guys, I'm taking off."

"Where are you going?" Emily asks.

"Out for dessert with a guy named Reece. We're walking down to Patty's."

"Okay, have fun and be safe," Kelsey says before wrapping her arms around me. "Happy birthday."

"Thanks, honey. I love you guys." I hug and kiss them both before walking back out to the bar and smiling when I spot Reece standing there waiting for me. "Ready?"

"Yep, lead the way."

We walk side by side down the street in a companionable silence. Up ahead I see Patty's, and when we step inside, we grab a booth toward the back. When the waitress comes to us, we both order apple pie à la Mode and coffee. A few minutes later, she returns with two huge pieces of pie with heaping scoops of ice cream and two cups of coffee.

"You are in for a treat." I dig in and take a huge bite, knowing I probably have ice cream in the corner of my mouth, but I'm rocking a nice buzz, so I don't really care, moaning and groaning around the pie as I chew it.

He takes a bite himself and closes his eyes. I know that look—pure ecstasy. "This is the best fucking pie I've ever eaten."

"I told you, didn't I? This place is an institution." I add cream and sugar to my coffee and take a generous sip. We finish our pie—well, I only ate half, and Reece finished mine as well as his.

I've never had this much fun talking to someone I just met before. It doesn't hurt that there's this underlying sexual tension that seems to be building between us.

I notice his lingering glances at my lips when we talk and the subtle glances at my chest. I, of course, have been checking him out too. When the check comes, I wrestle it away from him and pay it before he can. "I invited you for dessert, it's the least I can do."

Our waitress brings us a couple of to-go cups with coffee, and after I doctor mine up, we step outside. Right there on the street, Reece surprises me by cupping my face and pressing his lips to mine. The kiss is soft and tender, and my lips begin moving against his. He licks the seam of my lips and I allow him entrance into my mouth.

His kiss turns firm and seductive, and I swear I could come right now from this alone. Far too soon the kiss is over and he's slowly pulling away. "Fuck, if I didn't want to do that all night."

"Me too." My voice has taken on a breathy tone.

Reece reaches out, stroking my cheek so tenderly my eyes drift shut. Goosebumps break out across my skin as he whispers against my ear, "Come back to my hotel room with me?"

I've never had casual sex before. I've had two lovers, and both were about as inexperienced as I am. I feel like Reece is my one shot at spontaneous, uninhibited sex. "Okay," I whisper as my eyes open and find him so close, his breath hits me in sweet-smelling puffs.

With one more addictive kiss, he laces his fingers with mine, and hand in hand we head to his hotel. Neither of us says anything as we enter the lobby and step onto the elevator. We reach his floor and walk toward his door. He produces his keycard and slips it into the slot, but before he opens it all the way, he turns to me.

"We don't have to do anything. We can just hang out. I just wanted you to know that before we go inside."

Maybe it's the beer or maybe it's the sugar high from the pie, but I move toward him and place my hand on his chest, letting it slide up around his neck. I pull him down until our lips touch in a soft kiss. He pulls back, and I smile at him before pushing his door open and pulling him inside.

The door shuts quietly, and I turn to face Reece. In two steps I'm in his arms and my back meets the wall. I wrap my legs around his waist and feel his hard cock. His lips are on mine, and I open my mouth to his seeking tongue. Mine meets his in that familiar dance and I moan into his mouth as I feel one of his hands cup my breast, plucking at the nipple through my bra.

He sets me down on my feet and pushes my duster off. Then it's my shirt. I return the favor and slowly unbutton his, kissing every newly exposed inch of his chest. What a fine chest it is. All muscles and smooth skin that's totally kissable. I finally slip his shirt off his shoulders, and it floats to the floor. Then in one smooth move, I'm up in the air and then my back is hitting the mattress with Reece following me down.

Our lips connect in a fiery gnashing of lips, tongues, and teeth. My bra is gone in seconds and his lips begin their descent toward my breasts. He nibbles and sucks every inch of my skin as he makes his way down first to one nipple, sucking it between his lips. I grip the top of his head as a moan rips from my lips. He moves to the other, nipping it with his teeth and then sucking the sting away.

I whimper as he pulls away until I realize it's so

he can pull off one boot and then the other. He grabs my leggings and panties, pulling them down my legs until they're off. "Fuck me, you're beautiful," he whispers reverently. "Spread your legs for me."

Slowly I bend my knees and then let my legs come apart. I feel open and vulnerable, but it's a huge fucking turn-on. He grabs my thighs and spreads my legs even further. He leans in and I moan as I feel his tongue lick me from the bottom to the top, paying extra attention to my clit, sucking it between his lips.

"Oh God, that feels so good." I don't recognize my own voice right now. "Yes, right there." He again licks me from the bottom to the top, moaning against my pussy. Reece pushes one finger inside of me, rubbing the elusive G-spot. I pump my hips but then he pins them down with his forearm.

He adds another finger and begins rubbing my G-spot again, and this time he starts sucking on my clit with gusto. I reach up, pinching my nipples as I feel my orgasm coming. My head tips back as I arch off the bed, crying out.

"Fuck, you're squeezing my fingers." Reece pulls them out and then brings them to my mouth. I moan around them as I suck the moisture off. As he pulls them out, I nip at the tips. He pushes up on his knees and I reach out, unbuttoning his pants. As I pull the zipper down, nervous anticipation fills me when I see the outline of a very large cock behind the denim.

I look up at Reece. "Don't worry, he won't hurt you." Then he freaking *winks* at me and I can't help it—I start to laugh.

He grabs my sides and begins tickling me. I'm squealing and squirming until he finally stops and we're chest to chest. His gaze is intense as he strokes my cheek. "Are you ready for me to fuck you?"

"Yes, please." He grabs his wallet out of his jeans and pulls a condom free, tossing it on the bed next to me. Reece stands up and shucks his jeans, socks, and boxer briefs, and when I get the first look at his dick, my pussy involuntarily spasms. It's long and veiny, with the perfect girth, and my mouth waters at the sight of it.

He grabs the condom and slides it on, then settles between my legs. He kisses me urgently, sucking my tongue into his mouth. I feel Reece reach between us and line his cock up with my entrance. He pulls his mouth away. I hold his gaze as he slowly eases his big, beautiful dick inside me until he's buried to the hilt. We groan in unison before he slowly eases out until just the tip remains, and then slowly pushes it back in.

My thighs cradle his hips as he moves slowly in and out. He puts his arms under my thighs to lift me a little, and then he begins to drive into me with a force that has me crying out over and over. "Rub your clit, baby—take yourself there. I'm gonna come so hard."

Reaching down in between us, I begin rubbing my clit as the desire to come becomes overwhelming. I know that when I *do* come, it's going to be amazing.

As Reece pumps his cock in and out of me, he

bends his head, sucking my nipple into his mouth as something snaps inside me. He covers my mouth with his hand as I scream, "Oh fuck!" over and over until he plants himself deep and groans against my neck.

He collapses on top of me and I welcome the weight of him. I wrap my arms around his shoulders as his hot panting breaths hit my neck. I whimper as he pulls out of me. "I'll be right back." Reece kisses my lips before climbing off the bed and disappearing into the bathroom.

I'm not sure what to do here, so I get out of bed and search the floor for my clothes. Arms wrap around me and lips meet my neck. "I'm not done with you yet."

Turning in his arms, I look up at him. "You're not?"

Placing his hands on my ass, he lifts me with ease until I've got my legs wrapped around his hips and my arms are around his shoulders. With his lips on mine, he carries me back to bed.

***

I open my eyes and silence greets me. I stretch and moan as the evidence of my night reveals itself—my muscles deliciously ache and I can't help but smile. After Reece carried me back to bed he fucked me, and fucked me hard. We took a nap, then we woke and I rode him until we both came again. He and I fell asleep in a tangle of arms and legs.

Rolling over, I'm surprised to find the other side

of the bed empty. I reach my hand out and it's cold. Sitting up, I listen to see if I can hear him; maybe he's in the bathroom. I get out of the bed, and when I look around, that's when I notice his suitcase that was on the other bed is gone.

"Would he really leave without at least saying goodbye?" I whisper.

In the bathroom, I see a towel on the counter, but nothing else. Disappointment hits me like a freight train. I feel like a slut right now. I let a stranger fuck me ten ways from Sunday and when he was done with me, he took off…asshole.

I get dressed, and in the bathroom, I wash my face. Thank God I don't wear a lot of makeup. I use a little bit of the complimentary body lotion on my face. There's no toothpaste, so I just rinse my mouth and then pop a piece of gum into my mouth. After throwing my hair up into a knot on the top of my head, I grab my purse and pull out my phone. "Shit." It's dead.

Downstairs I ask the concierge to call me a cab and wait outside in the brisk air for it to show up. Luckily the cabbie isn't a talker, so I can stare out the window and mentally kick my ass for going home with a stranger to just be used by him, but isn't that what I wanted? A night of casual sex? Maybe I wasn't ready for it like I'd thought.

Twenty minutes later, the cab pulls up in front of my apartment building. Climbing out, I can't wait to hop in the shower, throw on some jammies, and curl up in bed. Before I can even stick my key in the lock, the door is thrown open. "Where the fuck have you been?" Brandon looks pissed.

"Um...I was out?" I step inside and he follows me to my room. Jose is standing in the doorway of Brandon's room. "Hey Jose."

"*Hola,* birthday girl." He looks behind me. "Brandon, let her do what she needs to, and you can talk to her after."

"No, I told you we'd be back last night, and when we get there, I hear you've left with some man you met at the bar. I tried calling you, but it went right to voicemail." He places his hands on my shoulders. "I was really fucking worried. I would've called the police, but that one threatened to withhold sex if I did."

I move toward him and wrap my arms around his waist. "I'm sorry I scared you. My stupid phone died, but that's still no excuse."

He looks me up and down. "Go get cleaned up, and then I want to hear *all* about the man that gave you love bites and whisker burns all over and has you walking like you were kicked in the imaginary balls."

"I love you."

He squeezes me tight. "I love you too. You're *lucky* I love you or I'd kick your ass." I watch him disappear into his room with Jose and close his door.

I really should shower because I smell like Reece, and after how he left, I don't really want to have that reminder. But instead, I crawl into bed and close my eyes. I hope I never have to see that douchebag again.

Chapter Four

Reece

Present Day

"It's you." I stand up from my chair and do a full perusal of Lilah's body. My eyes dart down to her belly…her *pregnant* belly. I meet her eyes, expecting to see anger because of how I left her that night, but instead I see a flicker of something subtle before her face goes blank. "How are you?"

The muscle in her jaw ticks as she walks around me to the table and sets the folder down. "Mr. Meyers, I'm Delilah Mackenzie, the office manager. I need you to fill out these forms and then return them to the basket outside of my office. I'll also need a copy of your insurance card, private investigator's license, and driver's license. Carrie can help you with that. Any questions?" She rests one hand on her belly and the other on her hip.

I don't remember her being this sexy, but I can't think of that now. "Is that…*my* baby?" Sweat dots my forehead and my pulse races. Throw me into a war zone and I'm cool, calm, and collected, but waiting to find out if I'm her baby's father has me ready to freak out.

Lilah—no, *Delilah*—looks at me with fire in her eyes. "No, it's *my* baby." She's out of the conference room, slamming the door behind her faster than I can say, "boo."

I slowly lower myself into the chair and rest my head in my hands. It's my baby, I know it is. The timing is just right for when we slept together.

That had been the most fun I'd had in a long time—the sex was phenomenal, and yeah, I knew she wasn't that experienced, but I hadn't had a clue how young she really was until I woke with her curled up against me. She just looked really young—*too* young for me once I came to my senses. She's probably still in her early twenties.

Meanwhile I'm thirty-four years old, moody, and kind of a loner. She's young and full of life and optimism. But no matter what, I need to get her to talk to me. That's my child she's carrying—I know it. We need to decide what to do.

Fuck, but I may be dead soon, anyway. As soon as Jack learns that I had sex with his daughter and somehow managed to knock her up, he's going to kill me and throw my corpse into Lake Michigan. In other words, it may not matter if that baby is mine because I may not be around to see it be born.

I should've woken her up before I left, plain and simple, but she'd been sleeping so hard that I showered, dressed, and packed and she never budged. I then debated on leaving her a note, but then I was a stupid dick and decided not to. Hey, I never said I was smart.

Grabbing the folder with the papers in it, I step into the hall and find Delilah's on the other end of the office. I give a quick knock before pushing the door open, but I freeze when I find Jack sitting in a chair across from her desk. "Oh...hey, Jack."

"Hey, Meyers, I see you've met my daughter. Luckily she looks like her mom." He looks at Delilah with a smile on his face, and then turns back to me. "Did you need something?" He looks at the folder in my hands and then up at me.

"Uh...yeah, I just wanted to ask Delilah here if she needed these papers back today or if I could take them home and fill them out."

"Go ahead and take it home with you. Why don't you come with me and I'll introduce you to Egan, and you can sit with him for a little bit? Del, he'll bring the papers in the morning."

Her cheeks and chest turn a dark pink and I can tell she's pissed. She slowly stands up. "Dad, I really would like those papers today."

"Honey, you can get that shit from him tomorrow."

She looks at me with fire in her eyes and then back at her dad. "You hired me to be the office manager. Let me do my job."

"Don't worry, I'll get them filled out and back to you before five," I say.

Jack nods and then kisses his daughter's cheek. "You're right, honey. I'm sorry." He moves to me and we head out into the hall. "You'll have to forgive her. The hormones have been a joy to deal with, but I love my girl."

Yep, I'm a dead man.

After spending the last few hours filling out paperwork and talking to Egan, I'm getting ready to head out. Jack left a little bit ago, and we're meeting the rest of the team in an hour. He's really big on all of us getting together often to foster that brotherhood mentality.

From my place in the hall, I can see Delilah is still here. She's alone, so I grab the paperwork to give to her.

When I knock on her open door, I don't miss the over-exaggerated sigh that leaves her lips. Fuck me, she's cute. "Here you go. Everything is filled out, and I put a copy of my insurance and license in there as well." I scrub a hand over my head. "Listen, I want to apologize—"

She cuts me off. "Listen, we don't need to talk about this. What happened, happened. We're both mature adults, I'm sure we can manage to work together without any drama, and no one needs to know what happened between us."

"They'll know, because that's my baby." I move closer to her, but she stops me, holding her hands up in a halting gesture.

"How do you know that this is *your* baby? Maybe I'm a huge slut that slept around a lot."

I chuckle, because that's pretty fucking hilarious. "I hate to tell you, but I'm really good at reading people, and I would've never have brought you back to my hotel room if I thought you were easy."

"Okay, yes, it's your baby, but that doesn't change anything."

"Why? I would like to help you. I'd like to be involved if you'd let me."

Her eyes drift over my face. "Why isn't this freaking you out? Most guys would run for the hills if their one-night stand produced a baby."

"Sweetheart, you'll learn that I'm not like most guys."

"Yeah, I can see that." Her lip twitches, but I can tell she's trying not to let that smile happen.

"Can we maybe get together and talk? I know we've got time before the baby comes, but I want to be a part of things. I've got to go meet up with the team right now, but just know that whatever you want or need, I'm there. It took *both* of us to make this baby."

"I don't understand how you're being so calm and rational about this. I've always figured that if we ever ran into each other that you'd freak out."

"I guess when you've seen and done the things I have, then your ability to get freaked out goes away. Although the only thing that scares the shit out of me is what your dad is going to do to me when he finds out. I see a shallow grave in the middle of nowhere in my future." Her lip twitches again but she tries to fight it.

"We'll cross that bridge when we come to it." She grabs her purse and messenger bag and then walks toward the doorway. "Have a good night, and welcome to the team."

"Do you need me to walk you home or whatever?"

She shakes her head. "No, but thanks."

Once she's gone, I sit in one of the chairs across

from her desk and scrub my hands over my face. "I'm going to be someone's father," I whisper. "Why is this not freaking me the fuck out...*seriously*?"

Chapter Five

Reece

I walk into the Chop House steakhouse and up to the hostess station. I don't miss the way she checks me out, looking me up and down. She's gorgeous, I'll admit—with her long, sleek, red hair and her tight black dress that hugs her hourglass figure—but it's images of a pregnant blonde with big brown eyes that assail me. "Can I help you?" she practically purrs.

"I'm here with the Mackenzie party."

"Yes, of course. Follow me." I don't miss the exaggerated sway of her hips as she leads me to the back. I find Jack, Erik, Marcus, Tyler, and Coby all sitting around a table.

I thank her, and she sashays away. I don't miss that they're all checking her out. I laugh as I pull my chair out. They all greet me, and I order a beer when our waiter comes over.

Coby is sitting next to me. "So how was your first day?" he asks. "I know it's always that first-

SECURITY BREACH

day bullshit. I heard Del got attitude with Jack in front of you. Those two are so much alike. That wasn't the first time, and it won't be the last."

Coby doesn't know that I'm the one who basically instigated the fight, unintentionally of course, but the love Jack has for his daughter was obvious. Since I already signed my contract, I don't think he'd be able to fire me when he finds out I'm the father of his future grandchild...can he?

When our food comes awhile later, I dig into the porterhouse I got and savor each bite. Conversation is nil as we all stuff our faces. Our waiter comes to take our dishes. Taking a drink of my beer, I turn to Coby. "I hear you're taking me to the range tomorrow."

"Hells yeah. I hear you're a great shot."

I hate to brag, but I was a top-ranked marksman. But hell, who knows—I haven't been to the range in a while, so maybe I'm a little rusty.

When they bring the check, Jack refuses to take money from any of us. He claims this is my welcome to the company dinner. While he waits for the slip, Erik and I make plans for me to come take a look at his Impala.

Jack answering his phone brings all our attention to him.

"Hold on, Brandon—*what?*" His face turns red and he shoots up from his chair, putting us all on alert. "Brandon, slow down. She what? *Goddammit!* I'm on my way."

"Boss? What's up?" Marcus moves to stand next to him.

"S-Someone attacked Delilah. Brandon had to

call 911. I've got to get to Rush." It's like the strong man I know is no longer with us. Jack looks terrified, and to be honest, I'm trying not to freak out myself.

We lead him outside and all hop in Tyler's Navigator. He maneuvers through traffic to get us to the ER. I don't know who this Brandon is, but I damn well will find out. It feels like forever before we're pulling up in front of Rush, and Tyler is tossing his keys to the valet.

I'm sure we're a sight—six large men barreling through the doors and heading toward the information desk. The woman looks up at us and blinks, dumbfounded. "C-Can I…I help you?"

"My daughter was brought into the ER. Delilah Mackenzie."

She taps away at her computer while Jack clenches and unclenches his fist. "Okay, yes, she's still in the ER. Take this hall all the way down to the end. They should be able to direct you to her."

We move down the hall until we reach the desk and they direct us to her in the back. I'm glad the other guys are along—otherwise it would look suspicious if I came back with him, because as far as he's concerned, I met her for the first time today.

Police stand in the hall and Jack walks right up to them. "I'm Delilah's father. Did you catch the motherfucker who touched her?"

"Mr. Mackenzie. I'm Officer Stevens, and my partner and I were the first on the scene. Whoever attacked your daughter was scared off by her roommate and his partner. We haven't been able to get too much information from her yet. They wanted to check the baby since she took a fist to the gut."

Nausea pools in my belly. Yes, we barely know each other, and I just found out that I'm going to be a father, but she and my baby were innocent victims. What kind of pussy motherfucker attacks a woman—a *pregnant* woman at that?

We wait in the hall while he goes in, but before he closes the curtain I see Delilah lying there with a fat lip and a swollen eye. The guys around me curse, and I know that they saw her too. Shutting out the noise in the hall, I try and hear what's going on behind the curtain.

"Baby girl, what happened?"

"H-He j-jumped me outside of m-my apartment building. D-Daddy, he s-said that it was y-your fault. He said that my baby was a mistake."

I don't need to be in the room to feel the supercharged air. Jack comes out a minute later. He pulls us down the hall away from the police officers. "What do you need from us?" I ask.

Jack looks wrecked as he turns to all of us. "Reece and Erik, I want you to canvass the area around her building. Check any security footage. My girl is smart—she says he's maybe six-foot-one, six-foot-two. He's Caucasian with dark brown eyes. A Cubs hat was on his head, so she can't tell me what color his hair was. Marcus, I want you looking through old case files, anyone that we may have pissed off, ex-husbands, ex-employees…whatever. I want this fucker found before the cops find him."

He tells us that he's staying until they get Delilah settled on the maternity floor. They want to monitor the baby overnight since she took a blow to the stomach. Just thinking about it makes my anger rise. Fuck, I want to go in and check on her, but I don't really feel like it's my place.

Plus, I want to wait until she's out of the hospital before I tell him that I'm the father of the baby. I know I should let her do it, but the longer we wait, the worse it will be. Now is definitely not the time for that, though.

***

By the time we had a game plan, none of the businesses by Delilah's apartment were open, but Erik and I plan to meet up in the morning. Egan and our other IT guy, Kyle, went to the office to see if they could hack into the city's traffic cameras.

Marcus is at the office already going through files and making up lists of possible suspects. I've been sitting outside the hospital for the past half hour, trying to work up the courage to go in there and check on her—check on the baby. I know Jack left already and was heading to the office. Twenty-five minutes ago her roommate left, and I may only have a short window.

"Suck it up, asshole," I mutter. Taking a deep breath, I go inside. After stepping onto the elevator, I stand quietly, watching the numbers light up as the carriage climbs higher and higher. Once I reach the floor, I walk slowly down the hall and ring the bell to get on the unit.

"Can I help you?" the feminine voice asks from the speaker.

SECURITY BREACH

"I'm here to see Delilah Mackenzie." The doors open and I walk in to the birthing center, stopping at the desk. "What room number is Delilah Mackenzie in?"

"She's in room sixteen. It's to the left and first door on the right."

On my way to her room, I pass the nursery and I stop to look inside. There are two babies in there in those clear plastic beds. All my life I never expected to have kids—they just didn't interest me. My baby sister has two of them, and sure, I've held them and played with them, but then I give them back.

The baby closest to the window yawns widely and an unexplained emotion fills me. My feet become unstuck and I make my way down the hall. I reach her door, knocking softly. Stepping inside, the lights are down low and the TV is on. The strong scent of cleaning solution fills my nostrils.

"Reece? What are you doing here?" Rage fills me when I look at her battered face. We may be virtual strangers, but she's carrying my child, and her father is someone I highly respect. I move toward the bed and have to fight the desire to place my hand on her stomach.

"I wanted to see how you're doing. I wanted to see how the baby was doing."

She leans over in bed to push a button and a fast *whoosh, whoosh* fills the room. "That's his heartbeat." I stand next to the bed, closing my eyes and listening to that beautiful sound.

I look at her with a raised brow. "*His?*"

She nods. "It's a boy."

"Wow. A boy." I know wonderment fills my

voice, but then I look at her face and remember what happened to her. "What did the doctor say?"

She rests her hands on her small belly. "They're keeping me here overnight just to make sure I don't start bleeding or contracting, but so far I'm okay."

"I'm glad. We're going to find who did this and make them pay." I say it with conviction because we will. We'll find out, and I *will* destroy him.

"Do you need anything? Can I go get you some food or something?" That feels like something so small, but for now that's all I can do. "We need to tell your dad that I'm the father. Sooner rather than later."

"No, I don't need anything, but thank you, and you're right. I need to tell him, but you need to know he may possibly kill you." Her eyes—or rather, the eye that's not swollen, twinkles.

"I'm prepared for that...I think."

"Hey girl, I've got your..." I freeze and turn around to find her roommate. He comes toward me. "I'm Brandon, and you are?"

"Reece." He shakes my hand and then goes to Delilah, bending down and kissing her cheek. Brandon whispers something to her. They turn to look at me and I don't miss the way her friend checks me out.

"So *you're* the baby daddy." He turns to look at Delilah. "You're going to have one good-looking kid. Way to go, girl." She giggles, but then sobers quickly, touching her face. My anger returns in full force.

I move close to the bed and look at her, then her belly. She nods and I slowly reach out, placing my hand on her stomach. It's soft but firm, and just as I'm about to move my hand away, I feel a little bump against my hand. I look at Delilah with wide eyes and she gives me a soft smile.

"He's really started moving to where I could feel it over the past few weeks," she says. "Little bumps here and there. He loves when I sing to him."

"Del's got the voice of an angel," Brandon says from behind me. "Sing to the baby now, Del."

She shakes her head. "I'm not your trained monkey." Delilah yawns widely. "I'm sleepy."

I should leave and let her rest, but who's going to protect her if the guy who attacked her comes back? Brandon seems like a nice guy, but he's not going to be able to stop someone who has no problem hitting a pregnant woman.

Brandon sets books, a bag of Skittles, and a package of powdered donuts on the table next to the bed. I look at them, and then at her with a raised brow. Her cheeks turn an adorable shade of pink. "This baby has given me a major sweet tooth. Normally I'm a pretty healthy eater."

"She is...she's also a pseudo-vegetarian, but the baby has her eating red meat like crazy," Brandon adds. "Girly, I'm going to head out. I'll be back in the morning." He leans down, hugs Delilah, and then gives me a wave before disappearing.

"You don't need to stay. I'm sure you've got stuff to do." She grabs her phone and starts messing with it.

I move across the room and sit on the couch, getting comfortable before staring up at the TV. "Sorry, sweetheart, but someone jumped you, hit you. I'm honestly surprised your dad didn't hire someone to sit outside your room. I can't in good conscience leave you alone. This is nonnegotiable."

"What do you mean, nonnegotiable? You can't just come in here and boss me around." She huffs and crosses her arms over her chest.

"Whether you want me involved or not, that's my baby you're carrying, and I'll do whatever I have to do to protect you both. I promise that to you."

Delilah doesn't say anything; instead she nods her head, settling into the bed. It isn't long before I watch her eyes slowly drift closed. She looks so young lying in the hospital bed. The bruises are purple and angry looking as I stare at her like a stalker. When I'm finally face to face with the guy who hurt her, I'm going to have a good time making him pay.

I'm a light sleeper, so when my eyes start to drift closed, I let them.

***

My eyes drift open, then closed, before popping open. Jack is standing over me. "You are *so* dead, motherfucker."

I jump off the couch. "Jack, I swear to Christ I didn't know she was your daughter. I didn't even know about the baby until yesterday." My hands go up in surrender. "You know me, man—I wouldn't fucking do that."

"Dad, please don't," Delilah cries from where she's perched up on her bed. Jack immediately goes to his daughter, wrapping his arms around her. "Don't be mad at him. I could've said no."

A nurse pops her head in, asking if everything is all right. We all tell her yes, even though she looks at us skeptically. I move toward Delilah and Jack once the nurse leaves. "Jack, you know me, man. I'll make this right."

"You're damn right, you're going to fix this shit! You guys need to get married."

My stomach turns, but Delilah speaks up first.

"That's not going to happen, Dad. When I get married I'm doing it for love. I'm sorry, but look at you and Mom. That was a nightmare for you, and granted I'm not her, but I don't want someone resenting me or my son because they think we trapped them into a marriage they didn't want. I know I'm young, and I don't know what I'm doing, but I'm sure now that Reece knows he'll do whatever he can to help, and to be there for us." She wraps her arms around him, and even though I know it's her dad, I get a little jealous. "Plus, I've got you. You're going to be the best grandpa there is."

It's easy to see how smart and put-together she is. Hell, less than twenty-four hours ago she was attacked, but she's calm, cool, and collected now. I admire her strength already. It also isn't hard to miss how much Jack loves his daughter.

Jack cups his daughter's face. "I promise I won't kill him, at least not until we've found the guy who hurt you. They said you could leave today, and I want you to come stay with me."

She's already shaking her head and opens her

mouth to speak, but I cut her off. "She can stay with me." They both look at me. "Jack, it makes sense. I've got a security system, and I just moved here—whoever did this doesn't know I work for you. At least not yet, and I can bring her to work every day, and take her home. I've got a spare bedroom she can sleep in. She'll be safe. Plus, she and I have lots to talk about."

Judging by the murderous look on his face, Jack has probably already killed me at least twice in his head. "You know I'm right," I say. "Let me do this. She's your daughter, and that's my son. I'd die before I let something happen to them."

"Daddy, he's right. I'm okay with it, and you need to be okay with it too."

"Fine, I'll arrange getting your stuff delivered there." He kisses the top of her head, and then signals me to follow him into the hall. "If you fucking hurt her or my grandson, I'll kill you."

"I wouldn't expect anything less. I meant what I said, man, I'll do right by them." I scrub my hand over my head. "Do I still have a job?"

He fucking *rolls his eyes* at me. "Of *course* you still have your job. I know you didn't know who she was, but, man…she's twenty-one, you're thirty-four, and I wanted her to get her life in order first before she started a family. I wanted to make sure all the poison her mom filled her head with was gone. That bitch convinced my daughter she was dumb and worth nothing for so long that sometimes Del is still too damn hard on herself." Jack shakes his head. "Stay with her while I make some calls."

Without another word, Jack takes off down the

hall. For a minute, I just stand there processing the fact that even though he's pissed—rightfully so—I'm still alive and employed. But *shit*...Delilah is *twenty-one?* I already knew she was young, but I'm a full thirteen years older than her, and she's having my baby. I pinch the bridge of my nose and groan. What the fuck did I get myself into?

I slip back inside the room and find Delilah in black leggings and pulling a tank top down, but I don't miss the quick flash of her rounded belly. A weird sensation runs through my body...lust, maybe...or love for my child? Whatever it is, it's quickly replaced with rage when she turns toward me and I see the huge bruise on the side of her belly.

Before I can stop myself, I'm right in front of her with my large hand covering her belly. "I swear to you that I'll make sure that you and our son are safe."

Delilah stares up at me. Her chin begins to quiver, and her eyes glisten. "I thought he was going to kill me," she whispers. "I thought I was going to lose the baby." A tear leaks from each eye. Before I can stop myself, I wrap my hand around the back of her head. I pull her until I can hug her tightly to my chest.

I rest my cheek on the top of her head. She cries softly against my chest. It takes her just a few minutes to get it out, and then she backs up, disappearing into the bathroom. When she comes out, her face is red. Maybe from wiping her face? "You okay?"

She nods. "Yeah, sorry for losing it."

I walk toward her, but she holds up her hands to stop me. Why does that one simple move rub me the wrong way? Before I can ask her what that was about, the aide comes in with the wheelchair to take her downstairs.

Delilah is certainly stubborn because she doesn't want to get in it, but finally she does and we head home.

Chapter Six

Delilah

It's been two days since Reece moved me into his home…temporarily. I swear it's the quintessential bachelor pad. The walls are bare. He's got a huge brown leather sofa and loveseat, which I will admit is amazing. The cushions are soft, but firm, and the leather is buttery soft. He's got his flat-screen mounted above the fireplace, and off to the side is some gaming device.

There is no kitchen table, but stools at the breakfast bar. Yesterday he went to the grocery store. Now the refrigerator is filled with fruits, veggies, almond milk, and eggs. He also got several options for breakfast, lunch, and dinner. I tried to give him money for the groceries, but he flat-out refused me.

Within two hours of being released from the hospital, Reece had my whole bedroom basically loaded up and transferred to his place. I do admit I love the neighborhood he lives in. It's quiet, except for the occasional child that can be heard playing or a random dog barking.

Another nice thing is my bedroom has a Jack and Jill bathroom that connects to the other spare room. I roll onto my back in bed with my hands on my stomach, smiling as I feel my son move around. Next week I have to follow up with my OB/GYN—she wants to make sure there are no lingering issues from the blow to my stomach.

Nausea pools in my belly as I think about the attack, and I fly out of bed, barely making it to the toilet. Over and over I empty the contents of my stomach. Hands pull my hair away from my face and then rub my back. When the heaving stops, Reece helps me stand up, flushing the toilet for me. He has me sit on the closed toilet, grabs a wet washcloth, and then wipes my face off.

"Morning sickness?"

I shake my head. "No, I was just thinking about what happened, and it made me sick."

He crouches down in front of me. "It's going to be okay, I promise."

The baby moves around like crazy. I grab his hand and put it on my belly, ignoring—or trying to ignore—the fact that he's in a pair of boxer briefs and nothing else. He's all sinewy, with broad shoulders, and I forgot that he had a light happy trail that disappears into his underwear, which outlines his big, beautiful cock.

Our son feels like he's doing cartwheels in my belly, and I know he can feel it because he looks at me with a huge smile on his face. "That's incredible. Does it hurt you when he does that?"

SECURITY BREACH

"No, but I've heard that as he gets bigger it'll feel more uncomfortable." I don't miss how his hand practically covers my entire belly. My breasts begin to tingle and feel heavy. If I stick my hand in my panties, my fingers will be wet.

That's been the one side effect of my pregnancy that's sucked because I'm single: I'm horny all the time. Before my last birthday, my libido had been almost nonexistent ever since I first started having sex. I was beginning to think something was wrong with me, but then I met Reece and realized it was just the partners I'd picked before him.

At the beginning of my pregnancy I was sick all the time, so I didn't think about sex too much, but a month and a half ago the morning sickness left and I became a hornball. I've had dreams so vivid I've woken up coming, and let us not forget the masturbating. I've been to the adult toy store by my place so much lately that the owner and I are on a first-name basis.

"Delilah?" His deep voice pulls me from my horny stupor. "You okay?"

I can only nod because it's possible I'd give myself away if I spoke right now. He stands up, and my mouth waters—his bulge is right in front of my face. I shove my hands under my butt so I'm not tempted to touch him, because my body is screaming at me right now to pounce.

"I'm going to go take a shower, and then I'll make us some breakfast." He disappears, and I take a deep breath.

The scent of him is all around me as I stand up. It's warm and woodsy with a hint of sweat. My body is like a live wire, but I ignore what I want and brush my teeth. Back in my temporary room, I stick my head out the doorway and hear his shower on. Quickly, I shut my door and grab the backpack that holds my toys.

I grab just my simple vibrator because I'm sure I don't have much time. Crawling under my covers, I strategically stick the vibe in my underwear so it's right against my clit. Closing my eyes, I think about Reece and our night together. It was the last time we had sex before I fell asleep.

His cock slips from my mouth with a pop, and I take the condom from him, sliding it down his thick shaft. My pussy is so wet right now I should be embarrassed, but I'm not. I straddle his hips and slowly ease myself down onto his cock. We groan simultaneously as my ass settles against his upper thighs.

Slowly I ease myself up and down, rolling my hips on each downward motion. My body does a full shudder each time because he hits that spot deep inside of me. My hands rest on his stomach for balance, and his fingers pluck my nipples.

The only sounds that can be heard are the wet squelches of my body and our pants and groans. Reece pushes himself up and wraps one arm around my waist. The other grabs my hair at the base of my skull. He uses it to bring my lips down to his, and he kisses me so hard I groan into his mouth.

I continue to slowly ride him until we're both worked into a frenzy. He flips me onto my stomach and pulls me up by my hips, thrusting inside of me so hard my head flies back and a moan rips from my lips.

"You're so fucking tight." He places a kiss between my shoulder blades. *"You feel so fucking good, baby."* My pussy likes him calling me "baby" because it spasms around him, causing Reece to groan. *"Fuck, I love that. Shit, you were made just for me."* He pulls me up until my back is against his front, and he begins to thrust into me over and over.

His lips touch the side of my neck while he rubs my clit with one hand and pinches a nipple with the other. The moment his teeth sink into my neck I come with a surprised cry. He follows me shortly after, and I fall face down onto the mattress with him landing on top of me. I relish the feel of his body on mine, but groan as he pulls out.

I slap my hand over my mouth as I begin to come. My pussy is trying to pull an imaginary cock inside of it. When it's over, I remove my hand and turn off the vibrator. Fuck that was so fast, but so good.

After quickly washing and putting away my vibrator, I put up my hair in a bun and take a quick shower. My dad wanted me to take the rest of the week off, but today I have to work on payroll. If he messes with it he'll ruin it, so I really need to go.

I put on some makeup—paying extra attention to my bruises with some concealer—and then throw on a fitted sundress with a cardigan over it. After slipping on a pair of nude ballet flats, I head downstairs. The scent of sausage hits me, and my mouth begins to water. It's very hard to eat every bit of meat this baby makes me crave, but it's only temporary.

In the kitchen, I find Reece at the stove in a pair of worn jeans that mold to his spectacular ass. The t-shirt he's wearing is fitted, but not so tight I can see every bit of six pack.

"Hey," I say as I grab a mug and pour myself coffee. Before I can take a sip, he takes it from me. "Um…that was mine."

"Coffee isn't good for the baby."

"*Seriously?* I can have one cup, it won't hurt him. Since when did you become a pregnancy expert?" From next to the stove he holds up a copy of *What to Expect When You're Expecting*, and all I can do is roll my eyes. "Well, my doctor says one cup won't hurt him, so give it back." I march right over to him and grab my mug.

He slaps eggs, sausage, and some buttered toast on a plate and sets it in front of me with a clatter. "What crawled up your ass? It's just a cup of coffee—hell, most of the time I drink decaf."

Reece comes toward me and bends down so we're face to face. "Next time you're going to masturbate, keep it down, and don't fucking moan my name when I'm not in there with you and there's not a damn thing I can do about it."

He stomps away, and my face heats up. I thought I was quiet, and when I came I covered my mouth…oops. It's not my fault he's so fucking sexy, and I know how well he uses his cock. I'm only human.

While I eat I wonder what it'll be like co-parenting with Reece. Would we live together?

What if he got a girlfriend? I don't think I could listen to him fuck some other girl, or worse he left to be with her, leaving us alone. I shake my head because there is no sense in thinking about that stuff until there is reason to.

After finishing my breakfast, I run upstairs and brush my teeth. I'm not sure where Reece is when I come back down, so I quickly pack my lunch. I start to put a lunch together for him but realize he probably wouldn't want that. Most of the guys go out to lunch.

I grab my phone off the charger and see a missed text from my mom. Ugh, I don't want to read it, but I'm dumb.

Mom: You finally get smart, and get rid of that mistake?

My stomach turns as I read her words. How can she be like that? Was it so terrible to have had me when she was young? Dad helped the best he could but serving in the military took a lot of his time. My mom would always try to poison my mind about him. She'd tell me that he didn't love me and didn't want me—that I was the reason he joined the Army and left us in the first place.

I knew it wasn't true because when my dad was home I was all he focused on. He made me feel like I was his whole world, and still does. It wasn't until I moved to Chicago that my dad told me the truth about my mom. My dad had tried to get custody of me so I could live with his parents, my grandparents, to get me away from my mom when I was ten. At the time I had let it slip that my mom had me on a diet because she said I was getting pudgy.

He had surprised me that weekend, and he happened to show up when Mom was in one of her moods. She was informing me how I dumb I was, and that I needed to work on my looks because when I was older that was the only way I was going to get a man. Dad made me sit in my room while they screamed at each other.

When Mom found out he was trying to take me away from her, she told him that she'd take me and run—that he'd never see me again—so as always, my mom got what she wanted—me, and my dad's money.

Of course, I didn't tell my dad that I already knew about him trying to get custody of me, and what Mom did.

Delilah: Hello Mother. It's nice to hear from you too. Yes, I'm very excited to be a mother. Your grandson is cooking nicely.

Mom: Just when I think you can't get any more stupid you surprise me. I'm no one's grandmother. You're ruining your life, and the poor shmuck's that you tricked into getting you pregnant.

I should block her number, but I don't. No matter what, she's my mom and I love her, even though she fucking hurts me every time. Why doesn't she love me? I wipe the tear that slips from my eye. I hate that she does this to me, and that I let her. I know Dad told me to never engage her, not until she could be nice, but I keep hoping she'll change. Maybe I *am* stupid.

My phone gets pulled from my hand. Reece looks at the screen, and I see his jaw clench. I quickly grab it from him, shoving it in my bag. He opens his mouth to speak, but I turn on him. "Don't. It's not your business."

I head outside and stand next to his car. He comes out and opens the door for me, and I climb in. We're both silent the whole drive to the office, and I'm thankful for that. I'm not even sure I'll tell my dad she reached out. I'm always afraid that one of these days she's going to push him too hard, through me, and he'll finally do something about it.

We get to the office, and again neither of us speaks as we ride the elevator up to our floor. As soon as Carrie sees me, she comes around the front desk and pulls me into a hug. Well, a sort of hug since our bellies are getting in the way. "Are you okay? I wanted to come check on you, but your dad wouldn't say where you were."

"I'm sorry. I'm staying with Reece since he just started. If whoever attacked me knows the people who work here, they shouldn't know him." Reece disappears into the back.

"Egan says Reece is the father of your baby." I nod. "You'll have to tell me that story later."

In the back I head to my office, and it's well past lunch before I finally get a chance to eat. I've had a steady stream of the guys checking on me. The only one who has been scarce today is Reece.

I know the guys have all been curious about Reece and me, but they luckily haven't asked. My dad probably asked them not to. Speaking of my dad, he's standing in the doorway to my office. "Hey, honey. Are you doing okay?" I nod. "Reece said your mom texted you spewing her bullshit again."

Of course Reece told. He's going to kiss my dad's ass to keep him from killing him for knocking me up. "It's not a big deal. I just ignored her." I know he doesn't understand why I still answer when she calls, and why I don't block her, but I just can't.

"If she contacts you again, you tell me. Okay?"

"Yeah, okay." I sigh. "Was I really that terrible?"

My dad's pissed—I can tell. "Never. You are the best thing that ever happened to me. Yes, we were young, but from the moment I knew you were coming I loved you so much. The moment the doctor put you in my arms, you stopped crying. Yes, I was scared as hell, but I was so fucking happy to have you. As far as your mom goes, her parents weren't nice people, and they taught her the same."

That statement right there scares the shit out of me. "What if I become her?" I whisper, my voice cracking.

"Baby girl, that's ridiculous. You've already shown this baby so much love, and he's not even here yet. I have complete faith that you're going to be the best mother." I get up from my desk, coming around to hug my dad.

"Thank you. Thank you for not killing Reece."

He laughs softly. "I don't like it, but he's a good man. He's had my back more times than I can count, and I've had his. I just have to accept the fact that he's the father of my grandbaby, and that he can handle the task of keeping you safe." Dad kisses my forehead. "I'll let you get back to work."

Reece doesn't come back to the office until it's time to get me. The ride back to his place is uncomfortable, and I don't know why. I didn't do anything, and he can't still be bent out of shape because I masturbated this morning. It can't be because I didn't want to tell him about my mom, either.

After he pulls into the garage, I climb out and grab my bag. He hasn't given me keys yet, so I follow him into the house and head up to my room. I quickly change into a pair of red knit shorts and a black ribbed tank top. In my bathroom I wash my face, brush out my hair, and braid it quickly.

My stomach growls and I head downstairs to start dinner. Reece is a pretty healthy eater, so I cook chicken, mixed vegetables, and quinoa. When it's finished, I sit down at the breakfast bar and eat…alone. By the time I'm done, he's still not back from wherever he went. I clean up the kitchen and decide to look in the garage to see if his car is gone. It's still there, but the motorcycle that was on the other side is gone.

Sadness washes over me, and I don't understand why. We had one night, and he didn't even stick around. I'm only staying with him now because it's safer. I'm the mother of his baby, but I don't think I mean anything more to him. Why would I?

Ugh...No pity party.

My mood deteriorates quickly, so it may be safe for everyone if I just go to bed. In my room I stack my pillows, snuggle into bed, and open my Kindle. I immediately get lost in my story. I love it: they were high school sweethearts and they split after an accident. When they're reunited a few years later, he finds out that she has a child, but it's not his. She won't talk about it.

I've cried multiple times already. It's not long before my eyes feel heavy.

***

A loud crash has my eyes flying open. I lie very still, trying to hear anything, but I don't. I go to sit up, but a hand covers my mouth. I scream against the hand and start fighting the person. They pin me to the bed and straddle me. My head thrashes around as I try to get loose to scream. The mask-covered face gets close to mine. "Delilah! Delilah, wake up."

My eyes pop open, my light is on, and Reece is sitting on the edge of the bed, looking at me with worried eyes. I put my hand over my racing heart and curl into a ball. My son is moving around like crazy inside of me, and I know for him I need to calm down.

I feel Reece's hand on my back. "Are you okay?"

"Y-Yes. I thought I heard a loud crash, and then someone's hand was over my mouth. H-He climbed on t-top of me and held me down."

SECURITY BREACH

"Sweetheart, there was no crash—no one was in here. You were screaming in your sleep. When I came in here you were thrashing in bed."

From my position curled up on the bed, I nod. "Thanks for waking me up." I roll over until I'm facing him, resting my hand on my exposed belly. "The baby didn't like that." Without thinking I grab his hand and place it on my bump.

Reece is incredibly good-looking, but when he feels our son move and smiles, he's breathtaking. His thumb strokes my skin back and forth, but I don't think he knows he's doing it.

"I'm sorry I snapped at you this morning. My mom is not a very nice person and has made it her mission to hurt me over and over again. From the moment she learned I was pregnant, she's been on me to have an abortion." Reece's hand tenses on my belly. "That was never a thought. No matter what, I wanted this baby."

"I'm sorry too. I know I've been off today. It's not you, I swear. There's just a lot to take in and deal with right now. We haven't found any clues yet to who attacked you. Erik and I have been everywhere looking at surveillance tapes, and we only have one that we caught a glimpse of him, but he's smart and kept his head down." He scrubs his free hand over his head. "You're safe with me. Even though I was gone earlier I had eyes on the house, and the system was on."

"Where did you go? You just left." It takes a second to realize that my hand is resting on top of his on my belly.

"I went to work out, burn off energy. I'm sorry I

didn't tell you I was leaving. Thank you for dinner. I ate some when I came back, and it was delicious."

"You're welcome. I'm glad you enjoyed it." I cover my mouth as a yawn slips out, and I'm disappointed when Reece stands up. I already miss the warmth of his hand on my belly. "What time is it?"

"It's nine-thirty. Do you think you'll have a problem falling asleep? I can make you some tea."

"I'm exhausted. I shouldn't have any trouble falling back asleep." I stand up and quickly realize I'm only in my tank top and panties. Reece's eyes devour me, and my nipples harden under his gaze, but he clears his throat, says goodnight, and runs like his ass is on fire.

I use the bathroom and brush my teeth before turning off the light and climbing back into bed.

It's a couple of hours later, and I'm no closer to falling asleep. Maybe I *should* make a cup of tea.

I climb out of bed and head silently down the stairs to the kitchen. While the water boils, I stare out the back window. I grew up in a town similar to this—quaint, and quiet. This is the perfect place to raise a child. I can totally picture our son running around the backyard.

Hands slide around my waist, causing me to jump, but in the window I can see it's Reece. I turn in his arms so my belly is pressed tightly against him. His gaze holds mine, and my heart races waiting to see what he's going to do. I want to bury my nose in his chest. Reece's scent is addictive.

"Can't sleep?" His voice is rough with drowsiness. I must've woken him up. He *is* a military man, so I'm not surprised he's a light sleeper.

"No." I don't know why I whisper. It's just us.

Reece starts to slide his hand down my back until he's cupping my ass. My breathing speeds up as I place my hands on his bare, hard abs. His hand flexes on my butt cheek, and I moan softly. His cock is rock hard—I can feel it poking me in my belly.

I lick my lips and watch Reece's face descend toward mine. At the last minute the damn tea kettle whistles and ruins the mood. He steps back, tells me goodnight, and disappears upstairs, leaving me horny, confused, and frustrated. I shake it off because it's probably not a good idea for us to do anything. But he can't possibly deny that there's some sort of connection between us that's undeniable…I felt it too.

After making my tea, I take it up to my room.

Chapter Seven

Reece

I'm in fucking hell. Delilah has me walking around with a constant hard-on. It's been a week since I almost foolishly kissed her in my kitchen, but fuck, she looked sexy standing there. Knowing that if she turned around I'd bear witness to her swollen belly, I never thought I'd find pregnancy sexy, but maybe it's because she's pregnant with *my* baby.

I've never jerked off more in my life. Every morning I wake up hard and want nothing more than to go crawl into bed with her and remind her how explosive we are together in bed. It's becoming more than just physical. I'm finding that I really like her. She's funny, witty, and mouthy, but in an appealing way. Even though she works for her dad, she doesn't act like it.

Delilah is constantly busy, doing what needs to be done to have everything run smoothly. It's impressive, and she's so much smarter than she gives herself credit for. All of the men respect her, and not because of her dad. She's *earned* their respect. I've seen the guys talking to her in her office like they're old buddies. It actually makes me a little jealous, which is ridiculous.

Today she has a doctor's appointment, and I'm going with her. It's a follow-up from her attack. She said we'll probably get to hear the heartbeat, and maybe actually see the baby during an ultrasound.

Later today I'm finally going to tell my parents about Delilah and the baby. I'm sure they're going to be happy because I'm happy. Sure, I never expected to have children of my own, but now knowing my son will be here in a few months is surreal.

I've been reading every book I can get my hands on, but while trying very hard not to tell Delilah what to do, not after the morning I took her coffee from her and I thought she was going to maim me. I really hope that she'll allow me to be there when he's born.

Co-parenting books are mixed in with the pregnancy books I bought. We've yet to talk about that stuff, but we should talk sooner than later. It would be best for us to have a game plan set. She doesn't have to worry about me getting married to someone else, or anything, but what about her? She's young, and beautiful. She deserves and needs to be with someone her own age.

Not someone who has no intention of getting married. I'll support her and our child even when she meets someone else, but I'll be damned if my son calls another man, "Dad." Fuck, I'm already marrying her off to someone else.

I pull into the parking garage and find Erik leaning against his Explorer, waiting for me. He's become a good friend. "What's up?" I say as I shut my door and meet him at the rear of his Explorer. We do the obligatory handshake-back slap combo.

"Nothing—I had the surveillance footage enhanced, but they couldn't get any more of a clear look at his face."

That's not what I wanted to hear. "Shit, that's not the news I wanted."

"I know. I'm sorry, man. How is Del feeling?"

"She seems to be okay. I'm here to pick her up for an appointment with her doctor."

He nods as we head to the elevator. "I still can't believe you're the baby daddy. We were all taking bets to see how long it would take for Jack to kill you."

"Yeah, I thought for sure he'd kill me that morning at the hospital, but I'm keeping his daughter and future grandson safe."

He turns to me as we wait for the elevator to open. "Do you see you and Del becoming a couple?"

I shake my head. "Not at all. She's too young for me."

"Good to know."

I freeze and turn to the elevator I didn't hear the doors open. Delilah stares at us with so much hurt in her eyes that my stomach twists.

"Delilah—" I say, but she cuts me off.

"Just save it, Reece." She walks past me.

I start to follow her. "Where are you going?"

"To my appointment." Delilah keeps walking, so I follow after her. Erik yells, "good luck," and I shoot him the middle finger.

"Come on, let's get in my car. I was planning on driving you. I wanted to be there." She looks ready to argue with me. "Plus, it's for your safety."

That does it, and she reluctantly follows me to my Mustang. I open the door for her then shut it before climbing in. I decide not to say anything for right now. The last thing I want is to upset her before her appointment. We reach the clinic ten minutes later, and I follow her inside. She gives them her name and then sits down next to me.

She types away on her phone, ignoring me completely. My eyes wander around the office, and a redhead across the waiting room gives me "Come fuck me" eyes. I'll admit she's beautiful, but she doesn't hold a candle to the woman currently ignoring me. I turn to look at Delilah and see she's staring daggers at the redhead.

When they finally call Delilah's name, I follow her into the back where they do all of the normal vitals, her weight, and blood pressure. In the exam room, Delilah sits on the table and the nurse has her lie back. The nurse exposes Delilah's belly, squirts some jelly on it, and then places a microphone-looking contraption on the jelly.

In a matter of seconds, the most beautiful sound fills the room. The rapid whooshing sound makes me smile like a loon. I grab Delilah's hand and squeeze it. I try to hold onto it, but she pulls her hand from mine.

Fuck me, I screwed this up royally. I just didn't

feel it was Erik's business until I know for sure what the fuck is happening between us. She doesn't have to be happy with me right now, but she at least will let me continue to keep her safe.

After the doctor comes in and pokes around on Delilah's belly, they bring us down the hall to a room with an ultrasound machine. The tech comes in and again covers Delilah's stomach with the clear blue jelly. The monitor gets turned toward us, and there he is…my boy.

Tears cloud my eyes as the tech shows us that he's got his fist tucked under his chin. We watch as his legs curl up, and then straighten out, like he's stretching. "It looks like everything is okay with this little one. We'll have Dr. Stephens take a look at this real quick, and if she clears you, we'll set up for your seven-month checkup. After that, you'll start coming in twice a month."

She disappears out of the room, and I grab paper towels to wipe Delilah's belly off. I'm shocked she *lets* me. "Thanks."

"Will they give us copies of the pictures? I'd like one if it's possible."

She nods. "Yeah, I'm sure they'll give us a copy."

The doctor comes in. "Well, baby looks great. Placenta is where we want it to be. He is measuring big, so we may do another ultrasound when you hit eight months, just to keep an eye on the baby's size. Here are some pictures for you to take." She hands them to me, and I look down. There's a great profile picture that I'll have to send my parents and my sister.

"Thanks."

"I do recommend you get signed up for the birthing class. We'll get you a list of the classes you can take. Are you Dad?"

"Yes, ma'am."

She shakes my hand. "Well, we have a class for first-time dads too. You guys take care, and Delilah, we'll see you in a few weeks."

"Thank you, Dr. Stephens."

We make our way out to the reception desk, and they hand us a folder that's filled with pamphlets for all the classes the hospital offers. All of this has made the pregnancy more real, for me at least. She's had lots of time to get used to the idea.

As we make our way through the hall we're again silent. Once we're outside, I spot the redhead standing outside talking on her phone. She spots me and hangs up on whoever she was talking to. "Hi."

I give her a chin lift but keep walking. It takes a second to realize that Delilah isn't next to me. She's in front of the redhead and looks pissed. "Are you *kidding* me right now? You didn't see that he's with me? It's not like I'm hard to miss."

The redhead flips her hair back with her hand. "Honey, if I want him, I'll have him."

"You know what—go for it. He's all yours." Delilah stomps away, and I'm speechless right now. She seems so sweet and quiet, but it looks like she's got that Mackenzie temper. I've seen her dad go from calm to busting faces in the blink of an eye.

Before I can react, she's in a cab that takes off down the road. "Fuck!" I take off in a jog toward my car. I call Jack and let him know what happened.

"Sorry Reece, she's just like her old man. What happened?" I tell him, and he starts laughing. I'm not sure if that's a good thing or a bad thing. "That sounds like my girl."

"She hopped in a cab before I could stop her. I'm not sure if she's going back to the office." I wait for him to chew my ass, but he doesn't.

"Listen, she probably went to Brandon. I'll ask him to text me when she shows up. My daughter may have a temper, but she's a good person. She's caring, compassionate, strong-willed, and stubborn. Delilah had a shit childhood, and there was nothing I could do because I was deployed. How any of that monster who birthed her didn't rub off on my daughter is beyond me."

"I told you last week her mom texted her, and I only caught a little bit. She asked her if she got rid of her mistake yet. I think that's been on her mind."

Jack curses, and then sighs. "I'm calling that bitch tonight. The nasty texts need to stop."

"Do you think that's a good idea? Couldn't this backfire and come back on your daughter? Sorry man, but you picked a real winner."

"Hey I was young, stupid, and horny. Becky did a great job hiding the crazy from me, until it was too late. I'll never regret my daughter, but I'll always feel guilty that she had a shitty excuse for a mother. Delilah isn't going to be like that."

"I know I don't know her well, yet, but I can see that. There's no question in my mind that she's going to be an amazing mother to our kid."

"I'll text Brandon and let you know where she's

at when you get back here."

We disconnect, and I head back to the office.

***

I just got off the phone with Delilah, and she's going to have dinner with Brandon before she comes home. She seemed a little more relaxed and not angry anymore. Jack assured me she's safe and Marcus is keeping an eye on her.

I can't really imagine what it was like growing up with a crazy mom. My parents are the epitome of a happy couple. Over the years they've fought, but they never stayed mad long. They supported my sister, Rachel, and I in everything we did.

Dad was involved in the Scouts with me and coached most of my sports teams when I was growing up. Mom and Rach had their stuff too. Every year we always went somewhere fun for vacation, and even if it was just a camping trip, we had a blast. Sometimes we'd pack, jump in the car, and just go. That's everything I want to give my son.

I grab a beer out of the refrigerator and drink it down while I heat up some leftover grilled shrimp and rice. That's one thing I've learned about Delilah: she's a phenomenal cook. It's been nice having a home-cooked meal every night. I've tried to take over the cooking, but she likes it and won't let me.

Knowing how good it tastes, I immediately scarf it down. Thank fuck she's not here because I'm making myself look like a pig. I finish, rinse my plate off, and grab my cellphone and another beer before heading out to my back deck to call my parents.

My mom's bubbly voice comes through the line. "Hi, honey. How are you?"

Don't let her sweet demeanor fool you, because you hurt one of her babies and she goes into crazy mama bear mode.

"Good. How are things? How's Dad?"

I love that I can hear the smile in her voice. "Things are great. Your dad is good. He's actually at your sister's right now helping Tim hang some new blinds."

I take a deep breath. "There's something I want to tell you."

"Oh God, are you sick?"

"No, Mom. I-I'm going to be a dad." Silence greets me on the other end. Fuck, she's upset, which is the last thing I want. I decide to tell her everything…well, not certain details.

"That's wonderful news. Sure, I wish you were married first, but children are blessings no matter how they get here. Our first grandson." She makes a squealing noise that has me pulling the phone away from my ear.

"I'll text you the ultrasound picture. The doctor said he's measuring big."

"Yes, please send me a picture of him. You should probably tell her that you were almost ten pounds when you were born."

"Well shit," I mutter, because damn, I don't want to tell Delilah that.

"Hey! Watch your mouth, young man."

SECURITY BREACH

I smile and shake my head in exasperation. I'm almost thirty-five, and she still scolds me like when I was twelve. "Sorry. Delilah's only five-foot-three. I can only imagine what that's going to be like for her."

"Delilah? That's a pretty name. What does she look like? Is she pretty?" Of course she wants *that* info.

"She's got dark blonde hair, beautiful dark brown eyes, and she's petite but fit. She gorgeous, and she's sweet, funny, smart, and a great cook."

Again, silence greets me. I hear my mom clear her throat. "She sounds wonderful. I can't wait to meet her."

I hear a noise and turn to find Delilah standing in the doorway. Her eyes are wide, and I know she heard what I said to my mom. I watch as she disappears back into the house. "You'll get the chance. I promise."

We hang up, and I quickly text her the ultrasound picture of her grandson. Her response is a bunch of the smiley face emoji with hearts for eyes.

My sister has two girls: Lara is three, and Joy is a year and a half. They live in DeWitt and not far from my parents. Rachel's husband is her high school sweetheart. They waited until they both graduated from college before they got married, but as soon as they said, "I do," she started spitting out kids. Last time I talked to her, they were trying for another baby.

I lock up downstairs before heading up. Delilah's door is opened far enough that I can see inside.

She's standing in front of the full-length mirror with her shirt pulled up and tucked into her bra. My body reacts when I see her turn to the side, looking at her belly that in a little over a week already seems to be bigger. She rubs her hands over it lovingly, and I reach for the door knob but decide against it.

It's amazing that from behind she doesn't even look pregnant, but I'm sure that once the baby gets a lot larger that'll change. She looks at herself from all angles, and I'm not sure what she's looking for but she looks beautiful, and now my dick's hard. Delilah's killing me with the little booty shorts that she wears. For someone so short, she's got legs for days. I remember the feel of them hugging my hips as I slid in and out of her hot, wet pussy.

I squeeze it through my basketball shorts, trying to ease the ache. A groan slips past my lips when she whips her shirt up and off, so she's left in her bra and booty shorts. Did she hear me? I don't think so, because she doesn't react. I should walk away—this is bordering on super creepy. She pulls her ponytail holder out of her hair and shakes out her wavy locks.

My fists are clenched to keep myself from reaching for the doorknob, shoving the door open, and fucking her into oblivion.

Chapter Eight

Delilah

It's so hard to pretend I don't know Reece is watching me from the doorway. I had come up with this seduction plan when I heard him talking about me on the phone to whoever that was. I know this won't go anywhere, and I won't get my hopes up, but that doesn't mean we can't have fun.

I'm just so freaking horny right now, and if he doesn't fuck me I may scream. Oh sure, I could use my toys because they *do* work, but I have the real thing right down the hall. I know this is a slippery slope I'm traveling on, and I could very well fall for this man, getting my heart broken in the process, but I can no longer ignore this pull that I feel toward him.

Taking a slow, deep breath, I reach behind my back and unhook my bra. I let my bra drop to the floor and use all my might to keep from covering myself. My boobs are about a cup size bigger, and I honestly love them so much right now. They look like I got a really good boob job. I plan on breastfeeding, and I've heard horror stories about it destroying a woman's boobs, but it's an easy sacrifice to make.

I let my hands run up my body until I cup a breast in each hand. My nipples are so sensitive right now that I've come just from stimulating them. I pinch them between my fingers, moaning softly. I think I'm ready for him to know I know he's there. Licking my lips, I take a deep breath and turn around just as his phone rings.

"Shit," he whispers. Then the door to his room slams shut, and I can hear his muffled voice.

I flop down on my bed with a frustrated sigh. It's just never going to happen with us. As willing as I am, he's just not, and that's okay. I throw my tank top back on without the bra and peel off my shorts. The panties I'm wearing are little bikinis with a wide waistband that feels comfortable around the underside of my belly.

After crawling into bed, I lie on my back and stare at the ceiling. Why did I even try to seduce him? I heard what he told Erik—that he wasn't going to be with me, and I was too young for him. That's okay. I certainly had planned to do this alone before I saw him again. We can co-parent our son like two civilized adults. Lots of couples do it, and if he has a family someday—hopefully his wife will love my son and treat him right.

God, I am just Debbie Downer tonight. Normally I'm pretty much the "glass is half-full" kind of girl. I hate blaming it on the hormones, but what else could it be?

SECURITY BREACH

Rolling to my side, I tuck my hands under my pillow. Luckily it doesn't take long before the ever-present exhaustion I have consumes me, and I fall asleep.

I fly up in bed. My heart is beating a frantic rhythm in my chest. I wipe my sweaty forehead with the back of my hand. I know I was dreaming, but I don't remember about what. All I know is that I felt hopeless and scared. In the bathroom, I splash cold water on my face. Back in the bedroom, I lie down, but can't sleep.

Before I can stop myself, I walk silently out into the hall and down to Reece's bedroom. His door is open, so I pad in until I reach the side of his bed. He's on his back with a hand resting on his stomach and one tucked under his pillow.

"Reece?" I whisper. "Reece, can I sleep with you? I had a bad dream."

He doesn't say anything; he just lifts the blankets. I climb underneath and snuggle into him, my back against his front, and he wraps his arm around my waist. His large hand covers my belly. I'm surrounded by his natural warm scent and the faint hint of laundry detergent. In seconds his light snores fill the room.

Reece holding me lulls me into a dreamless sleep.

***

My eyes open, and it takes a second to realize that I'm in Reece's bed, and I'm alone. I slide my hand across the mattress, and his empty spot is cold.

It gives me a flashback to our night together, but I shake it off. I climb out of his bed and quickly make it before heading back to my room.

After a quick shower, I throw on another pair of knit shorts and one of my dad's old rock band t-shirts. AC/DC is stretched out across my belly, but the shirt is so worn it's nice and soft. Hopefully my dad doesn't mind that I stole it, especially since we're spending the day together later shopping for furniture for the nursery.

We haven't really seen a lot of each other since I was attacked, but that's only because he's been busting his ass trying to find the guy who hurt me. I know he and all the guys have been working double time looking for him, but the guy's a ghost.

I quickly braid my hair until it hangs over my shoulder in a thick plait. After slipping on some Nikes, I head downstairs and find I'm alone. I make myself some tea and a bowl of oatmeal. Settling into a seat on the back deck, I wrack my brain trying to remember the dream I had last night. All I know is when I woke up I felt so helpless.

How long will Reece keep me here? How long before I wear out my welcome? Through the sliding door, I can hear my phone ringing. I set my bowl down and step inside to grab it. "Hello?"

"Get rid of that baby or I'll get rid of it for you." The call disconnects and my phone slips from my limp fingers, nausea swirling in my stomach. Before I can collect my thoughts about what I just heard, the sound of glass shattering fills the house.

I scream and drop down to my hands and knees, scurrying across the cold tile flooring, heart racing,

SECURITY BREACH

until I make it inside the empty cupboard under the breakfast bar.

The scent of pine—and fear—burns my nostrils as I listen for any imminent danger, but I can't hear anything over my rapidly beating heart.

"Delilah!" It takes a second before I realize it's Reece calling my name.

I open the cupboard door, and he's there in seconds pulling me out and into his arms. Tears begin to flow as he tugs me to his chest. "What happened?"

"Someone called. T-They told me that if I didn't get rid of the baby, they'd get rid of it for me. Then I heard glass shattering, and I hid."

He cups my face. "You did good, baby." His thumbs brush my cheeks.

My dad shows up thirty minutes later, followed by half of his team. They take my phone to see if they can track the call. Then they start talking about what to do with me. It's obvious that whoever attacked me knows where I am.

As soon as my dad mentions a safe house, I put my foot down. "Dad, no, I need to be here. My doctor is here, my job is here. Carrie's going to have her baby soon, and I'll need to find her replacement. Who's going to keep you in line? Dad, *please* don't make me go into hiding."

My dad comes toward me. "Let's go upstairs, and talk."

I follow him reluctantly, and we step into my room. "Dad, please don't send me away."

He grabs my shoulders, raising an eyebrow as he looks down at my shirt—I mean, *his* shirt. "First, nice shirt." Hugging me tight, he mutters, "Nothing can happen to you. I can't lose you, and I can't lose my grandson."

"Whatever you need me to do I'll do, but please don't send me away."

Dad reaches out and places his hand on my belly. My son kicks his grandpa, and I smile up at him. He knows it's his papa. My dad was adamant that he be Papa, which I love.

"Let me talk to Reece and the guys. Just sit tight." He disappears downstairs, and I lie down on my bed. I don't understand why someone wants to hurt me and my baby. Who could hate my dad that much?

I'm not sure how much time passes before Reece comes into my room. He sits down next to my hip and places his hand on my belly. "You're going to keep staying here. Egan is going to install a more heavy-duty alarm system that'll tie into our office. They'll see everything in the perimeter. Someone will always be with you. When we're here, your dad has the police set up to do frequent drive-bys."

I sigh heavily. "I hate this. I've never hurt anyone."

He rubs small circles on my belly as he talks. "Sweetheart, it's not lost on me that you're a good person. Until we figure out who is doing this, we won't know the why. Your dad says you were supposed to go shopping for baby furniture today." I nod, bummed that I won't be able to go, but it's for the best. "I know it's not the same, but let's look online later. We'll see if we can find something we like."

I nod and push myself up to a sitting position. "Thank you." He holds my gaze then wraps his arm around my waist, pulling me toward him. That invisible pull has us moving closer and closer before his lips brush softly against mine. Our kiss is slow, and sweet. I open my mouth enough to let his tongue flick against mine.

All too soon he ends the kiss. Before he gets up, he presses his lips to my forehead. "I'm going to go talk to the guys, then we'll shop."

He disappears into the hall, and I place my fingers against my lips. They're tingling right now, and I want to kiss him over and over again.

I slip my shoes off since I'm not leaving, and head downstairs. Ugh, they all stop talking as soon as I enter the room. They end their conversation in quick whispers. I get hugs from everyone, and then my dad stops in front of me.

"Be smart, and listen to Reece. I'm going to find him, I promise." He kisses my cheek, and then he's gone. I don't want him burning himself out, but I can't tell him to stop. He wouldn't listen to me if I did.

I'm left hanging with Reece and Erik. We order pizza, hot wings, and breadsticks, and while we wait for the food to come we start looking at cribs. Hearing these two huge men talk about cribs cracks me up. They talk about design, color, what bedding would match. If I were smart I would've recorded them and used it for blackmail.

Reece and I decide on an espresso-finish crib. The back is higher than the front, and the edges are rounded and smooth. I pick the mattress, and then we pick out the bedding. The blueish-gray and cream bedding will go amazing with the crib. Before I can pay for it, Reece is entering his credit card info.

"Hey, I could've paid for that."

"I know, but I want to do this for my kid."

I can't be upset about that. "Thank you."

For now, we're going to set up the baby's crib in my room, just because we don't know how long I'll be here. His office is set up in the other room, so I don't want to disrupt that.

The pizza comes, and we sit in front of the TV while we eat. My cheese pizza is so delicious, even though I want to eat a huge slice of their meat lover's pizza. Once we finish, they board up the broken window. I guess while I was upstairs they cleaned the glass up.

"Jack's got a guy coming early next week to fix the window," Reece says after coming back inside. "Egan will be here tomorrow installing the new system."

"Okay. Is the new system going to be easy for me to use?"

"Egan won't leave until you feel comfortable using it. We're installing panic buttons in several of the rooms. That way if something should happen you just hit the button, and help will come."

I feel bad that there has been damage to his home, and now he's going to have holes drilled everywhere. While they watch a college football game, I curl up in the corner of the sofa and read.

Erik gets up and grabs a beer for him and Reece and a bottle of water for me. "Thanks." I take it from him. "Erik, what happened with that girl Carrie set you up with?" Carrie is our resident matchmaker. She's set up all the single guys, and even set *me* up on a blind date.

He leans back on the couch so his head is right by me. "Del, why are bitches so crazy?"

"Hmmm…could it be because you call us bitches? Carrie said she was totally your type—tall, legs for days, fake boobs, and collagen-inflated lips."

He laughs so hard he grabs his stomach. "Del, you are the little sister I never had."

"I'm going to tell Gretchen that." Gretchen is his fourteen-year-old half-sister. Erik's dad died when he was sixteen, and his mom married his step-dad, Tad. He was eighteen when his sister was born, and he's super protective of her.

"Har, har. No, this girl is the complete opposite of what Carrie told me. She's about average height and is all tits, hips, and thighs. Plus she's a brunette, and mouthy. We still went out, and our waitress may have flirted with me a bit, and I thought Shayla was going to drop the poor girl. After dinner I was going to take her to a show, but she pulled me into the alley and practically climbed on my dick."

He grins. "We got a hotel room, and let me tell you—we fucked all night long. All. Night. Long. We both passed out, and when I woke up she was gone, and my dick was sore. I haven't seen her since, and Carrie won't tell me where to find her."

I set my Kindle aside. "Didn't you call her, and pick her up for your date?"

"No. She told Carrie where I should meet her,

and what time. I've never clicked with someone the way I clicked with her, and then she just fucking used me for sex, and took off."

My eyes drift to Reece, and he looks at me with apologetic eyes. I give him a smile that I hope says that it's okay. I turn back to Erik. "I'm sorry. Maybe she got scared. Maybe she felt that strong connection too, and she got spooked."

"I don't know why I care," he huffs.

"Aww...you care because you like her."

He stands up, pulling me up with him to give me a hug. "Whatever," he mumbles. "Be smart, and make sure you're aware of your surroundings." I reach up and give him a kiss on the cheek. Reece gets up and follows him outside.

While he's having his man to man with Erik, I clean up the kitchen and wrap up the leftovers. Maybe I could get Reece to take me out tonight. Since I got attacked I only go to work, Reece's, and maybe Brandon's. Speaking of my BFF, maybe Reece would let me have him over for dinner one night. I miss hanging with Brandon and Jose. Hell, I miss all of my friends.

It's just so hard now because they're all in their early twenties, single, and ready to party. I'm almost seven months pregnant, and no fun at all. Now that I think of it, most of my girlfriends don't really talk to me anymore. I guess it doesn't bother me that much because I didn't even realize it until just now.

Growing up, Brandon was my only true friend— my mom scared off most of the friends I had tried to make by acting like a psycho, or hitting on their dads and pissing off their moms. For some reason Brandon was the only one she was nice to.

Reece comes into the kitchen and leans against the counter. He surprises me by reaching out and tucking an errant strand of hair behind my ear. "You doing okay?"

"Yeah, it helps knowing how hard everyone is working to keep me safe. Can we do something tonight?"

"Like what?"

I chew on my thumbnail; it's a terrible habit. "Maybe go see a movie? I just haven't done anything since the attack."

"Sure, but with one condition…no chick flicks."

A giggle slips past my lips, and it feels good. "It's a deal." We even shake on it. "I'm gonna head upstairs and get ready."

I throw on a pair of black leggings, a fitted white v-neck t-shirt, and my red Vans. My makeup is light—natural looking—and on my lips I've put on clear gloss. I don't want to look like I'm trying too hard or that I think this is a real date.

I grab my purse and head downstairs. Reece is sitting on the couch looking delicious as always…dick. His black t-shirt molds to his muscled chest. He stands up, and my eyes immediately drift down to the noticeable bulge in his pants. I look away quickly before he catches me.

"Did you pick a movie?"

"How about we see that new superhero movie?"

I nod. "That sounds really good." Of course that's a lie, because the *last* thing I want to watch while I'm horny—and can't do anything about it—

is hot, muscly guys who at some point will be shirtless.

After getting our tickets and snacks, we head to our theater. They've got the reclining leather seats here, and they're so comfortable. I recline my seat, but apparently Reece is too cool for that. We don't have to wait too long before the lights dim and the previews start.

After the movie ends, we head back to Reece's house. I'm about to head upstairs when he stops me. "Come sit with me. Let's talk." I take his hand, and he leads me to the sofa. "I talked to my mom and told her about the baby. She's really excited about being a grandma again."

"How many do they have now?"

He pulls out his wallet and shows me a photo of two adorable little ones. "Lara and Joy are my baby sister, Rachel's, kids. As you can see, they look just like her."

"They're beautiful. Are you guys close? I always wished I had siblings, but my mom could barely handle me, and I'm pretty sure she never wanted me in the first place." I realize what I just said, and cringe. "Sorry."

"Is that why she's been on you about getting rid of the baby?" I nod. He wraps his arm around my shoulders, hugging me into his side. "You have your dad, and it's obvious he loves you very much. Plus, you never know—she might change her tune once the baby is here."

"That's a nice thought, but I highly doubt it." I take a deep breath. "You're right, though. I'm lucky to have my dad, and he's obviously very awesome."

SECURITY BREACH

I look up at Reece. "I'm glad you've got good parents. At least the baby will have one full set of good ones."

"Maybe before you get too close to the end we can go see mine, or maybe they'll come here. My mom would like to meet you."

That makes me nervous. It's not like this baby was conceived out of love. It was obviously faulty condoms, but I don't regret it. "Did you tell your mom that it was a one-night stand gone wrong?"

"Not in so many words."

"She probably thinks I'm a whore."

He turns abruptly until he's looming over me. "She does not, and I don't want to hear that shit come out of your mouth again. That mother of yours put that into your head, didn't she?"

I can only nod because he looks super pissed right now. Reece pushes off the sofa and begins pacing like some caged animal. I get up and stand in front of him, halting him from pacing further.

"No matter what, I'll never regret being with you, and creating him." He places his hand again on my belly. I don't know what it is, but it does things to my insides when he does that. Our son likes it too, because he gives a little kick.

My eyes begin to burn, and then tears begin to leak from my eyes. "Thank you for saying that. Can I tell you something?" He wipes my tears away and nods. "As strong as I was trying to be, I was really scared at the idea of doing this all by myself. I mean, don't get me wrong because I know I wouldn't have been alone, but there's just something about knowing you'll be there that makes me feel good."

He hugs me tight. "I'm just sorry I wasn't here sooner, or that I took off without at least exchanging numbers." He kisses my forehead, and then rests his against mine. "Come sit, and I'll make you a cup of tea."

"Okay, thank you." I curl up in my spot and stare outside while I wait for him to bring me my tea. When he comes back a few minutes later, watching this big man walk toward me with a teacup in his hand makes me smile. He sinks down onto the sofa next to me and turns the TV back on. We start watching *Vikings* when I feel him pick up my feet and start massaging them.

Chapter Nine

Reece

In the past two weeks Delilah and I have fallen into a routine. In the morning, I get up early and work out in the basement, then I make breakfast. While she eats, I shower. We go to work, come home, she makes dinner, and then we hang out until she usually goes to bed. She's crawled into bed with me a handful of times, and while she sleeps next to me I stare up at the ceiling. Her body pressed up against mine always has me so hard I'm fighting the urge to wake her and fuck her.

Three days ago, Carrie and Egan became the parents of a little boy they named Leif. Holding him made me anxious to hold my son, but nothing beat watching Delilah with the baby cradled in her arms.

Jack has been in a terrible mood lately, but everyone's pretty much been on edge lately. We're still no closer to finding the guy who attacked Delilah. The phone he called her from was a burner...of course. Those are a little more complicated to trace.

I pull into the parking lot of Gus's Gun Shop and Shooting Range, and Jack's car is already here. I grab my case out of the trunk and make my way inside. Gus is about seventy and a retired Army general. He does a lot of the maintenance on our firearms.

"Hey, Gus. How are you?" I shake the man's hand.

He gives me a slap on the back. "I'm good, Reece. Jack's already in the back. Go ahead and head that way."

Gus buzzes me through, and I head toward the back. Jack's at a table messing with his Sig Sauer and Glock 17. "What's going on, Jack?"

"Hey, man."

I look him over and realize he looks like shit. "Are you sleeping at all? You know you're no good to Delilah if you're fucking exhausted."

"When you're a father you'll get it, so until then, I'll go without sleep, or food, and whatever else I have to do to find that fucker and to keep my daughter safe."

"Okay, I get it. She's worried about you, just so you know."

Jack stares at me for a second, and then turns back to his guns. "Are you and my daughter a couple now?"

It feels like we are, and I find myself missing her if she's not around. Even though I don't sleep when she's in bed with me, I still like it. Usually when she wakes me up, I pretend to be half asleep when I lift the covers. When I do that, she snuggles right into me. My bedding smells like the light floral perfume she wears, and every night I fight the urge to bury my nose in my pillow and jerk off.

I don't think it would help, though—I've tasted the real thing and I want more. We've kissed a few times, and they've been amazing, but I've been the one holding back. There are a lot of things to consider, and sure, we could fuck and it would be great, but it could also screw things up for us relationship-wise. I'm thirteen years older than she is. What if we get together and in a couple of years she wants to find someone closer to her own age?

It makes me sound insecure to have those fears, but if things went bad it could be difficult for us to co-parent, and that's the last thing I want. In the Army not much rattled me, but the tiny, pregnant blonde has me questioning everything.

I look at Jack. "No, we're not, at least not yet." Do I tell him that I'm developing feelings for her? No, I can't. Not until I tell her first.

He nods and then slips on his earmuffs, and I do the same. We spend a couple of hours at the shooting range, and Jack seems to be a little more relaxed when we pack up to go. I follow him back to the office. We head inside, and when we step off the elevator I see Delilah's sitting at the reception desk with Carrie's replacement.

The brunette is shooting daggers at Erik...Oh shit, that's the girl he went out with, and she ditched him. This should be interesting. Erik's sitting in the corner pouting and staring at her. Delilah shoots me an amused smile, then gives her dad a worried look. "How was shooting?"

"It was good," her dad says, and he disappears through the doors to the back.

I lean against the counter, lowering my voice. "You know he's not going to admit that he's burnt out. The guys and I will watch out for him. Don't worry, okay?"

"Yeah okay." Delilah's lips tip down in a cute pout. She stands up. "This is Carrie's replacement, Shayla. Shayla, this is Reece." Shayla reaches out and shakes my hand.

Erik stands up and he and I head to the back.

The rest of my day goes by fast. I took my first client meeting, and he's pretty well-known. He's a big entrepreneur and is convinced his wife is setting up a second life so she can take their kids and run. Before I took the meeting, I followed him and dug up any info I could find. I wanted to make sure he was a good guy before I did anything. Had the guy given me a bad vibe or been a dick, then I would've helped his wife free of charge.

It's time for me to show them what I can do. I lock up the file in my cabinet and then go out to reception to find Delilah. Instead, I find Erik sitting real close to Shayla. She's whispering harshly to him. She spots me and gets up quickly. "H-Hey. Delilah went to the bathroom."

I sit on the loveseat with my ankle resting on my knee. Shayla isn't even looking at Erik anymore, and he can't take his eyes off her. I'm curious about the real story. I don't believe half of what he told Delilah. There is so much more there than they're saying.

Delilah comes out with her purse and computer

bag. She stops at the desk. "I'll see you tomorrow, Shayla. You did great today."

"Thank you. See you tomorrow."

I grab Delilah's hand as we step onto the elevator, and thankfully she keeps holding it. I let go to wrap my arm around her shoulders and kiss her temple. By the time the doors open, her arm is wrapped around my waist.

We reach my car when what sounds like gunshots echo. I grab her, yanking us down with my back taking the brunt of the fall. Marcus comes running toward us. "You guys okay?" He reaches out and helps Delilah up first, then me. "It was a car backfiring. The hunk of shit is breaking down outside of the garage." I should've known that it wasn't a gun; I guess I'm more on edge than I thought.

I wrap Delilah in my arms and stroke her back until the trembling stops. Marcus pulls her away from me, grabs her by the back of her head, and leans in to kiss her forehead. I'd get growly if it wasn't anything other than a brotherly kiss. Plus, she still has a hold of my hand. "You're all good, honey."

She nods, and then I load her into my car. "Are you okay?"

"Yeah, but I'll be happy when this guy is caught." She fiddles with her phone.

When I look in the rearview mirror, I see a car following us. If he's trying to be slick, he certainly sucks at it—I made him the minute I saw him. I don't want to alert Delilah, so I gradually speed up. Thankfully she's oblivious to it. I pass a couple of cars and check my mirror. Okay, now he's gaining on me—maybe stealth hadn't been his M.O. from the beginning.

We play our own little game of *Frogger* as we travel down the highway. I spot my exit up ahead, but I don't want to get over until the last minute so we can lose them for sure. The only problem is it's kind of risky, and I don't know if I can take that chance with Delilah in the car.

At the last minute, I decide that I can't do it.

"Hey, you just missed our exit," she says.

I do my best playing dumb. "Oh shit, I'll take the next one." I accelerate, and with quick movements I weave in and out of traffic, managing to finally get over, take the exit, and lose them.

We take the long way toward my place just to make sure we're not being followed. When I finally roll into the garage and close the door behind us, I'm able to relax. "Let's just order out tonight. Does that sound good?"

"Can we have Chinese?" She loves Mongolian beef with extra water chestnuts, and can eat her weight in crab Rangoon.

"Yeah, the usual?" She nods, and I quickly call it in. Delilah heads upstairs, returning a few minutes later in shorts and a t-shirt, a freshly washed face, and her hair in a high ponytail.

When the food comes, we camp out on the sofa and watch *The Punisher* on Netflix. I'm surprised she chose it, but I won't complain. I was afraid I'd have to watch some shit like Full fucking House.

She moans around each bite, and I swear my dick is getting hard. When we finish we clean up and then snuggle on the couch as we watch a couple more episodes of the show.

Delilah stands up and stretches. Her t-shirt rides up on her rounded stomach, and I can't help myself—I reach out and touch it. She covers my hands with hers. "He loves Chinese." A thump hits my hand. Now that she's twenty-eight weeks, she's in the beginning of her third trimester, and according to the books I've read, she's really going to start popping out.

Every week her body changes—her breasts are beginning to spill out of her bras, but her belly is the only other thing that looks pregnant on her. From behind, you'd never guess. I just can't wait until her belly really starts moving. They say that sometimes you can see the outline of hands or feet.

"Are you gonna try going back to being a vegetarian after he's born?"

She shrugs. "I don't know. I guess it'll depend on the baby. I plan on breastfeeding, and as long as he gets the nutrients he needs then I'll go back to no meat. Of course inside me he's rejected tofu and most beans, so we'll have to see how he does on the outside."

Delilah picks up the trash and then heads upstairs to bed. I watch a little bit of the news, and then lock up before heading upstairs. I'm tempted to grab her and bring her to my bed, but I don't. Under my covers I reach for my aching cock, giving him a squeeze. This hard-on seems ever present when I'm around her…or think about her.

I close my eyes and drum up memories of our night together. Before I can start stroking my cock,

I hear a faint buzzing sound. I sit up in bed and listen closely. A faint moan hits my ears, and my dick throbs. She's masturbating right now. Fuck me, enough is enough. We both want each other—there's nothing stopping us.

On silent feet, I walk out of my room down to hers and listen at the door. Sure enough, the muffled buzzing can be heard. Delilah moans again, and I grab the knob and push the door open.

"Reece! What are you doing? I was—I was using a massager on my sore muscles." She scrambles to cover herself with her comforter, her eyes wide and panic written all over her face.

I don't say anything. I just walk toward her bed, and to my pleasant surprise, Delilah gets up on her knees, letting the comforter drop.

I swallow the lump in my throat because she's breathtaking. Her hair is down and around her shoulders. The tiny tank top she's wearing barely contains her breasts or her belly, and she's not wearing any panties, so her pussy is on display for me.

She holds her hand out to me, and I don't hesitate taking it and climbing on the bed. In seconds she's in my arms, and our lips connect in a sensual glide. My hands grip her hair at the base of her neck, using my hold to control the kiss…deepen it.

My tongue seeks entrance into her mouth, and she obliges me by opening hers, our tongues dueling in our own private dance. I let go of her hair as we kiss, and my hands drift down to the hem of her tank top. Easing it up, I let my fingers graze her

SECURITY BREACH

nipples and swallow her moan.

I pinch them between my fingers, and she grips my wrists as she pulls her mouth away to throw her head back and moan—loudly. My dick is leaking pre-cum and I don't fucking care, but if I don't get inside of her soon I'm going to lose it. My boxer briefs are the only thing standing between my cock and her snug, wet heat.

Letting go of one nipple, I reach down and rub her pussy. "Fuck baby, you're drenched." I slide my fingers through her wet folds before bending down to take one nipple into my mouth. I suck hard as I strum her clit. She grips my head and starts grinding against my hand. I move my mouth away from her nipple. "Are you gonna come, baby?"

"Yeeeeesssss," she moans.

I suck her nipple back into my mouth and shove two fingers inside her. She tightens around me immediately, crying out incoherently. "Oh, oh, *oh*." She moans as she rides my fingers. I bring my mouth up to hers, kissing her hard until the pulsating in her pussy stops. After pulling my fingers from her, I bring them up to her lips and paint them with her juices.

I lick her lips, moaning as her flavor explodes on my tongue. We kiss as I grab her hips and work her down on her back. Instead of coming down on top of her, I lie on my side up against hers. In the dark we stare at each other, and no words need to be spoken. She reaches down between us, palming my cock.

She uses the right amount of pressure that has me getting close to the edge before she backs off.

My lips graze her chin before grabbing it with my teeth. "It's been hell having you here, and not touching you, when I've wanted to every single night."

I bite a trail down her neck to the spot where it meets her shoulder. My teeth clamp down, and I feel her shudder. I keep thrusting into her hand, feeling my dick getting harder and harder. She pushes me until I'm lying on my back, and then peels my underwear off.

Delilah straddles my hips, her pussy resting on my dick. I use my arms to push myself up until she can bend down and kiss me, her belly pressed firmly against mine. She begins rocking against me, coating my dick with her wetness. "Put me in, baby," I whisper against her lips.

She rises up on her knees and wraps her hand around my dick. After rubbing the tip through her wetness, she lines me up and slowly lowers herself onto my cock. I groan against her lips when she settles in the cradle of my lap, my dick buried deep inside her snug channel. She begins to slowly rock back and forth and up and down.

I cup her face, and something important, something vital, passes through us. She feels it too because she does a full body shudder that has me groaning. Delilah begins to move faster, and faster, panting and moaning with each thrust. She's controlling everything right now, but I need to move. I need to come.

I reach between us and use my thumb on her clit until she grabs onto my shoulders and begins to rock her hips. "Oh God," she moans. "I'm so close." I wrap my lips around her nipple and suck hard, and she explodes around me.

When the ripples finally stop, she sags against me. Carefully, I flip us until she's on her back, and with my arms tucked under her knees I spread her legs as far as they'll go and thrust back inside. With fast, deep thrusts, I pound into her over and over. She cries out with each thrust, holding onto her headboard for purchase.

Her belly shakes, and for a second, I pause. "Am I hurting you?"

"No, please don't stop." I begin to pick up the pace and feel my balls tingle, knowing that I'm quickly going to come.

"You feel like heaven. I want to spend every minute of every day inside of you." I thrust twice more before I can't stop it from happening. "Oh fuck, baby. I'm coming." I empty myself inside her with three deep thrusts, not missing the fact that she comes too with a long, deep moan.

I slip from her body and lie down next to her, pulling her into my arms.

"That was amazing," she says before kissing the underside of my chin. She strokes my chest as we lie in silence. Right here is where I want to stay forever. It just feels right.

"I didn't use a condom, but I haven't been with anyone since you," I mutter.

She kisses my chest. "Same, and it's not like you have to worry about getting me pregnant." Delilah giggles—fucking *giggles* before burying her head against my chest.

I kiss the top of her head and place my hand on

her stomach. Our son moves around, and something dawns on me. "That wouldn't have hurt him, would it?"

"Ummm…No, not at all. He's protected pretty well in there. Will you stay with me tonight?"

I didn't want to assume anything, but I'm glad she asked. "There's no place I'd rather be."

Chapter Ten

Delilah

My eyes flutter open, and I feel a heavy weight at my back. A huge grin splits my lips, and I snuggle against Reece. His arm is wrapped around me, and it makes my heart flutter. He woke me in the middle of the night with his mouth on my nipple.

He ended up fucking me slowly, and thoroughly. We came together with long moans that I felt all the way down to my soul. I turn my head to look behind me, and see that Reece is sound asleep. God, he is the most beautiful man I've ever seen. I hope our son looks just like him. Of course I wouldn't be sad if my baby boy looked like me. I just want him to be healthy, and happy.

I grab his hand and bring it to my mouth. I kiss his palm and then set it on his side. Climbing out of bed, I moan. My body is deliciously sore, and I ache in all the right places. I grab his t-shirt off the floor, and when I step into the hall—I won't lie—I bring the material up to my nose, inhaling his familiar, enticing scent.

I drop it and step into the bathroom. After finishing, I brush my teeth and brush out my hair, leaving it down. In Reece's bedroom, I find that he's still asleep, so I head downstairs to make *him* breakfast for a change.

I'm in the middle of frying up some bacon when he wraps his arms around my waist. "Good morning," he says against my neck. I can smell the toothpaste he just used.

"Good morning. I thought I'd make you breakfast for a change." I turn my head and kiss his lips. "Do you want coffee?"

I move to get it, but he stops me. "I'll get it." He walks to the coffeemaker and I admire his shirtless back. The dips and swells of his muscles beckon me to trace my tongue along each line. His basketball shorts ride low on his hips, showing off two sexy dimples above an ass that would make David Beckham jealous.

When he comes back to stand next to me, I try very hard to control myself. He's got a six pack that leads to that glorious V that you see in men's fitness magazines. I want to drag my tongue across each nipple and bite them.

He lifts my face to look at me. "Are you okay? You look a little flushed." Reece flashes me a cocky grin and winks.

I smack him with the towel and squeal when he grabs it to pull me flush against him, kissing my lips hard. "Go sit, and I'll bring you your plate."

After we finished eating we both went upstairs to

shower. I'd tried to tell him we were showering separately since we had to get ready for work, but we ended up getting *really* creative in there.

Now as we make our way to the office, I lean my head back and a sense of contentment fills me as I stare out the passenger-side window with Reece holding my hand.

We reach the office, and he comes around to help me out. Hand in hand, we ride the elevator up to our floor. I figure he's going to let me go, but instead he keeps ahold of my hand.

Most of the guys are there, including my dad. They don't miss the fact that we're holding hands, but thankfully they don't say anything. "Good morning," I say in my extremely fake, chipper voice.

A couple of the guys laugh, and my dad grumbles something under his breath before kissing the top of my head. "I'll talk to you later."

I watch him walk away. The worry I feel swirls in my belly like acid, and I want to go after him, but the look he had on his face was the one that said, "stay away and let me be." Reece follows me into my office and shuts the door. "He's going to be fine." He kisses my lips softly before leaving me to my work.

By the end of the day I feel like I haven't gotten anything done. All I've been doing is worrying about my dad and trying *not* to worry about whoever has it in for my dad and is using me to do it. Shayla asked me to lunch but I declined, and being the sweet girl she is, she brought me a sandwich from my favorite shop.

On the plus side, Brandon and Jose are coming over for dinner this weekend. I really want Brandon to get to know Reece, and vice versa. I look at the time on my computer and see that it's almost six. I lock my computer, lock all of my files up, and grab my bag.

The office seems to be cleared out. I know there's someone here in the room in the back with all the monitors. I don't know the two guys who keep an eye on them during third shift very well, but when I only see them in the morning when I go in early—and that only happens for the monthly staff meeting—it's hard to play the "get to know you" game.

I forgot my phone so I can't call Reece, but wait…I head into my office and pull his file. I dial him using my office phone, but it goes right to voicemail.

"This is Reece." Typical…short and to the point.

"Hey, it's me." Wait, maybe he won't know who "me" is. "Um…me, Delilah. Are you picking me up? Call my office phone."

I hang up and wait…and wait, and wait. My stomach growls and I see that it's now six-thirty, and I can't wait anymore. I'm starving, and now crabby. I head to the elevator, take it down to the main floor, and head out the front.

The building's security guard gives me a warm smile. "Have a good night, Ms. Mackenzie."

"Thank you, Mr. Allen." I set out into the warm night and wait for the cab they said they were sending right away.

A few minutes pass before I hear that familiar

rumble and see Reece's Mustang turn the corner, stopping at the curb right in front of me. He hops out, looking a little frazzled. "I'm sorry. I was with Erik following a lead, and my phone died." Reece opens the door for me, but before I climb in I kiss the underside of his chin.

"It's okay. I was just so lost in trying to get stuff done at the end of the day that I lost track of time. When I came out everyone was gone, and then I remembered I didn't have my cellphone to call you. I had to look up your number from your file."

He strokes my cheek. "I forgot about your phone—no wonder when I called it earlier it went right to voicemail."

We settle into our seats and my stomach rumbles. "He's hungry," I say, rubbing my belly. We end up stopping to eat dinner at a little Mexican restaurant.

"Were the leads you were following about a new case?"

"Yeah, it's that guy who thinks his wife is setting up a new life without him somewhere. It's going to get messy before it's over."

When they take those cases, it always makes me sad because the couples had to be happy once…right? It makes me totally gun shy about ever getting married. Plus, look at my parents' marriage. Dad tried to make it last as long as he could, but he'd finally had enough. My mom used me as a pawn to manipulate him.

I don't think either one of them know that I know Dad tried to get custody of me, but Mom threatened to take me and run.

"Hey. You okay?"

I look up at Reece and shrug. "Yeah, it just brings up bad memories. My mom put Dad through hell. Things were so bad between them, even after they got divorced. She's mental and enjoys making our lives hell. I'm never getting married." I mutter the last part, and then smile at the waitress when she sets my food in front of me. "Thank you."

Neither of us speaks as we eat, and I'm thankful for the reprieve. My son can tell I'm upset because he gives me a little kick. What if I turn into my mom? I know I won't, at least realistically, but that kernel of fear lives inside me.

After dinner, we head back home—or Reece's home, I should say. I know I'm being quiet—distant, even—but thinking about my mom and my childhood has always done that to me. It's taken a lot of love from my dad and Brandon to help me deal and cope.

I slip off my shoes and head up to my room. I change into a cotton candy pink tank top nightgown. In front of the mirror, I look myself over closely. My mom and I could pass for twins, and when I was little she used to preen when people would gush how perfect we were. Little did they know living with her was hell on Earth.

A noise startles me, and I turn to see that it's Reece standing in the doorway. "You okay?"

I shake my head. He comes into the room and wraps me in his strong embrace. In minutes I feel more centered...relaxed. I pull back and look up into his eyes. "Sorry. I don't know what my problem is. I do think I'm going to bed. I'm tired."

SECURITY BREACH

"Grab your Kindle and come lie in my bed. I've got some stuff to do, but you can sleep in there." I do as he says and let him lead me down to his room.

His bed is a huge California king with the softest cotton sheets, big fluffy pillows, and thick warm comforter. All are the same dark gray color, and the frame of his bed is a grayish-looking wood. I never really looked at his stuff before, or maybe I just didn't really pay attention to it. He pulls back the blankets for me, and I climb up onto bed—settling in.

Reece bends down and gives me a kiss on the lips. "I'll be up in a little bit."

"Good night," I tell him before he disappears out into the hall. I turn on my Kindle and get lost in my fictional world.

***

"Do you need help with anything?" I look up at Reece from in front of the stove. I'm working on browning the ground beef for my lasagna. The noodles are on the stove in a pot of boiling water.

"Nope. I've got the filling all mixed together, the salad is tossed and in the fridge, and the garlic bread is buttered and ready to go into the oven when it's time."

He comes to me, rubbing my shoulders. "Wow. Okay, let me know if I can do anything." I feel his lips touch me right behind my ear, and I do a full body shiver.

It's been a couple of days since my "woe is me" pity party, and I'm feeling lots better. Reece has been great and hasn't brought it up, for which I'm grateful. Tonight, Brandon and Jose are coming for dinner. Reece offered to make himself scarce, but I want him to know my best friend and the godfather of our child. No matter what happens with us, I want him to know the people that'll be in our son's life.

After constructing the lasagna, I stick it in the oven and then head upstairs to change. Since it's just my boys tonight, I throw on some dark gray leggings and an off-the-shoulder red t-shirt that molds perfectly to the basketball in my belly. I pin my hair up into a knot and don't bother with makeup.

As I'm heading down the stairs I hear the doorbell, and when I reach the bottom Brandon and Reece are exchanging one of those manly back-slapping hugs. I giggle when I see Brandon rest his head on Reece's shoulder.

Reece is a good sport, patting Brandon awkwardly on the back. Jose finally has to intervene and pull Brandon off of my man—wait, *is* he my man? We really haven't clarified anything. Although the past couple of nights I've slept in his bed with him, we've only slept. Maybe he felt I needed space, or needed the time to get my head straight.

While Jose talks to Reece, Brandon comes toward me. "You look fantastic." He places both hands on my belly. "He's going to be a monster."

I slap his arm playfully, his green eyes twinkling at me as he chuckles. "My baby is *not* going to be a monster."

"I know, I'm just teasing. You look beautiful. I can't believe how much your belly has grown since the last time I saw you."

I rub my belly, smiling at him. Jose comes to me and kisses both of my cheeks. "Hey, doll."

"Hey, Ho."

Reece grabs drinks for everyone and then sits down next to me on the sofa. I lean into his side when he wraps his arm around my shoulders.

"So Reece, Del tells me you used to be in the Army with her dad."

"Yeah, we were both Special Forces. I enlisted when I was eighteen, and at first it was just because they'd pay for college. I just got out last year, and Jack had me come out to talk to him about a job, and well…we know how that story ends."

He looks at me and gives me a squeeze. My cheeks heat up as I remember that night. I do a full body shiver that I hope no one notices, but I couldn't get that lucky. Reece looks at me, his mossy green eyes flaring with desire…for me. I lick my lips—it's a nervous habit, and I don't miss the way he follows my tongue.

"Should we go?" I turn wide eyes to Brandon and Jose, who are grinning like lunatics at us.

It's then I realize that Reece's hand is in my hair, and he's leaning over me, our lips so close I can taste the beer on his. He chuckles before kissing me chastely and then sitting back up. The timer goes off. I excuse myself, and as I step out of the room I hear them all chuckle. Being the mature woman I am, I flip them all the bird, and of course they laugh louder.

Earlier this week Reece bought a dining room table, so we eat in the dining room. Everyone seems to be getting along and conversation flows freely, but Brandon's never met a stranger. Reece has been very touchy feely throughout, rubbing his hand up and down my back and pulling me by my head toward him to kiss my lips softly, but the best is when he just rests his hand on my belly.

After we finish eating, I clean up while they go out to the garage to look at Reece's car. A thought occurs to me: I'm going to need a car. I sold mine when I moved here because I take the L or an Uber everywhere.

I don't want to have to try and strap a baby carrier in and out of an Uber all the time. I could get something reliable enough to get me where I need to go and that'll keep the baby safe.

I wrap up the leftovers and am sticking them in the refrigerator when the boys come back in.

"Del, have you told Reece that I'm your kid's fairy godfather? Have you told him that the baby's middle name is going to be Brandon?"

I smile at my best friend. "No, I haven't." I place my hand on my belly. "His middle name will depend on whatever his first name is, and we haven't really talked about it. We start our child birthing class next week."

I told Reece that he didn't have to go, but he was insistent. He's been adamant about being in the delivery room when our son is born too, which makes me very happy.

"How fun," Brandon says, his voice laced with sarcasm.

SECURITY BREACH

I wrap my arms around his thin waist and hug him tight. "It will be, and we'll learn lots of useful things." I look to Reece. "I hope they don't show a birth. Blood makes me squeamish."

Brandon kisses the top of my head and then turns to Reece. "When we were about twelve, I tripped while we were walking home from school. My knee got tore up, and Del took one look at it and passed right out. I had blood running down my leg, but *I* had to carry *her* home." I nod because hell, it's true. "In high school, we went to donate blood, and she did fine when they stuck her, but she accidentally looked, and they had to hit her with the smelling salts to wake her up."

"I'd like to think I won't be like that with my own child," I grumble. Great, now I've got one more thing to worry about. Instead of letting it show, I plaster on a fake smile. "I guess we'll just have to see what happens."

When it's time for them to go, Brandon drags me outside to talk quickly. He places both hands on my shoulders. "I'm really, really happy for you. He's absolutely crazy about you."

"He likes me, but he's not *crazy* about me."

"Del, you know I love you, but you're blind. He never stopped touching you. He watched you with an intensity that we could all feel. When you practically started fucking on the sofa I felt like I needed a cigarette." His face turns serious. "Girl, I'm so fucking happy for you. After years of not being happy, or as happy as you could be, it's nice to see you smiling like you have been all night."

"I just don't want him to regret being with me

because I'm a lot younger than he is."

"Age is just a number. In the grand scheme of things, it doesn't matter. All you need to worry about is being a good mother, and being a good partner, co-parent, or whatever you and Reece decide to be. I know you didn't have a great childhood, and that you still carry the scars, but you are so strong. You survived that, so you can survive anything."

"I love you, Brandon. I don't know how I survived without you."

He gives me a squeeze. "You would've survived because that's what you are…a survivor."

Jose and Reece come out, and Jose kisses me goodbye. Once they leave, with his arm around my shoulders, Reece leads me inside.

***

Reece grips my hips as he powers into me from behind. "Oh God, right there, baby," I cry out. He's hitting a really good spot deep inside of me, and my body trembles. I'm so wet right now that I feel the wetness all over my groin and upper thighs.

He's already given me two orgasms—once with his fingers while sucking on my sensitive nipples, and then once with his tongue between my legs. I've never been a fan of oral sex, but Reece knows what he's doing and gave it to me so good, and then some.

My arms tremble as he picks up speed and then moans against my ear. "Get yourself there, baby."

I reach in between my legs and begin making

little circles around my clit. My moans turn to cries as I feel my orgasm coming on, and fast. "I'm coming," I moan.

His thrusts become brutal, but I relish the pleasure/pain I experience. My orgasm seems to last forever, and I'm vaguely aware of his groan as he plants himself to the root. Aftershocks shake me as I feel each blast of his hot cum inside of me. When we both finally start to come down, he pulls his softening cock from me. "I'll be right back."

I watch his gorgeous naked body as he disappears into the bathroom. He comes back with a washcloth and cleans me off. After he tosses it into the laundry basket, he climbs back into his bed and pulls me toward him, but my big belly gets in the way.

After sex the baby always acts like it's party time. Reece's large hand covers my belly, and he smiles so sweetly at me as we feel our son move around. "I love feeling him kick my hand," he whispers.

"I love it too. Except when his foot gets caught in my ribs, and Carrie says that toward the end he's going to love using my bladder as a kickball."

He leans forward, kissing my lips. "Let's get some sleep."

I roll over and he pulls me so that my back is up against his chest. I grab his hand, pull it up to rest in between my breasts, and let myself fall asleep.

Chapter Eleven

Reece

I step into the office after grabbing a quick sandwich. Shayla is behind the desk in reception, and for once Erik isn't hovering over her. She shoots me a big smile. "Hey, Reece! Jack wants to see you in his office."

"Thanks, Shayla." I head through the doors and find Jack sitting at his desk.

He looks up when I knock on the doorframe. "Hey Reece, come on in and shut the door." I do as he asks. "I wanted to give you an update on things, but first—how was Delilah's checkup?"

Delilah had her seven-month checkup the day before. "It went well. He's measuring big, but I was a big baby. I tell you what—I'll never get tired of hearing his heartbeat."

"I'm glad." He stares at me a beat. "I know I didn't react well when I found out you were the father of Del's baby, but I'm glad it's you."

I'm stunned speechless, and I don't know what

to even say or do. "I appreciate that. I care deeply for her."

"I know you do." He scrubs his hands over his face. "I wanted you to know that we've hit a dead end on Delilah's case. I'm honestly so fucking lost right now. Do I keep chasing dead ends, and pushing myself toward total fucking exhaustion? If I pull back the only thing that keeps me feeling okay with it is that she's got you protecting her."

"Of course, you've got me. Man, even if we're not together I'll always protect her and our kid."

"I know you will. That's why I'm glad it's you. I've just never been this fucking stumped. We've been monitoring her phone and there have been no calls, nothing."

Since the phone call and the rock through my window there's been nothing, and I'm happy about that, but a part of me is waiting for shit to fall apart. "Maybe since they know there's a whole team protecting her they gave up."

"Yeah, maybe. I've got another case I have to follow up on, and I'll be out of town for a week. I need to trust that you'll help keep an eye on things." Jack scratches the stubble on his chin. "Erik and Marcus will keep an eye on all ongoing business, Delilah can run everything else, and you—you just take care of my daughter."

"You got it, boss." I stand and salute him, but then I get serious. "I won't let anything happen to either of them. I promise."

Our workday ends at noon and Delilah and I decide to take lunch to Carrie and Egan. I know she's excited to get her hands on their baby. To be honest I am too. I need to practice changing diapers.

They live about ten minutes from the office in a nice apartment that looks like a huge house. Delilah practically sprints to their door, with me chuckling as I walk sedately behind her. Egan answers with their son in his arms. I know he's married, but I have to stop from growling when he kisses Delilah's cheek.

She takes the baby from his arms and disappears inside. "Hey, Egan. How are you?" I shake his offered hand.

He scrubs a hand over his dark blond hair. "I'm fucking tired, but I'm so happy. My wife is the shit."

"That's great, man." I clap him on the back before following him inside.

We find Delilah and Carrie sitting on the sofa, and Delilah is cooing at the baby. Carrie smiles up at me from the sofa when we enter the room. "Hi, Reece."

"Hey Carrie, how's it going?"

She smiles warmly at her son, and then up at me. "It's going great. I can't remember the last time I slept longer than four hours, but it's so worth it."

The plan was to order takeout once we got to their place, but another idea came to me on the way here. "I know the plan was to order takeout, but what if you guys went out to lunch, and we stayed with this little guy? You know it would give us a chance to practice." I hope they don't think this is because we don't want to hang out with them. "Or we could grab some takeout, and maybe you guys could go have a drink after we eat."

SECURITY BREACH

Delilah smiles at me. "Yeah, guys. Let us give you a break."

The couple look at each other and then back to us. Egan speaks up. "How about this—we'll go to this great pizza place that's about ten minutes from here. Carrie and I will have a drink and an appetizer. We'll order pizza to bring back for all of us."

After the new parents leave, I sit down next to Delilah. "Here, let me have him." Carefully, she places the little chunk in my arms. He's so tiny, but substantial. His eyes open, and he blinks at me. His balled up little fists go right to his mouth and he begins sucking on them. "He's a lot heavier than he looks."

I look up at Delilah, and her eyes are bright with unshed tears. "Hey, what's wrong?"

She shakes her head. "Nothing, you're just going to be a really good dad. I'm glad you're his father."

"I'm glad too."

The baby makes a wet fart sound. "I think someone just made a deposit in his drawers."

Delilah gets up, and I follow. We take him into his room and I lay him on the changing table. Together we manage to get his little sleeper off, and then he begins to cry. I take off his diaper and gag at the present he left for us. While I hold his little legs up she wipes him down, and then squeals because she gets some on her fingers. At the same time Leif begins to pee all over himself and me.

We both take it in stride, getting him and ourselves cleaned up. Delilah puts him in fresh pajamas and then picks him up, snuggling him to her chest. The boy is smart and knows he's got a good thing going when he snuggles into her breasts.

"Will you hold me like that later?" I whisper into her ear. She's so expressive when I touch her, and right now Delilah's doing a full body shiver. I kiss her cheek, and just as we get settled on the sofa, Carrie and Egan come in carrying a couple of pizza boxes.

"Hey guys, how was he?" Carrie takes Leif from Delilah.

While we eat, Delilah tells them about our two-person diaper changing sideshow. "We're going to need lots of practice," she says while holding her swollen stomach.

"Trust me, you'll become a pro quick. I could probably change Leif's diaper blindfolded at this point. Right, babe?" Egan smiles proudly at his wife.

"Of course. You're the master." He gives her a heated look, and I look away. Delilah saw it too because she's smiling at them and then me.

Even from across the table I can still smell Delilah's familiar scent. I can even smell it over the scent of tomato and melted cheese. She breaks the connection first by turning her head. It's not lost on me that her cheeks are flushed, and she's breathing heavier. The tension is broken only moments later when Leif decides he's tired of being ignored.

We leave a short time later. The baby was being a little fussy, so we said our goodbyes.

On the drive home, I grab her hand. "Have you thought of names yet?" she asks. "I've got a couple."

SECURITY BREACH

"Uh...not really. I just assumed that was your call," I tell her truthfully.

I glance at her as she shakes her head. "No, I want your input, totally." She squirms in her seat until she's kind of facing me, but still protected by the seatbelt. "I really like the names Sawyer, Parker, Maverick—"

"Wait, let me stop you right there. No kid of mine is going to be named Sawyer or Maverick. What is this, a soap opera?" I don't have to look at her to feel her glare on me. "I'm sorry babe, but I don't like those names. What about Mitch, Jake, or even Reece Jr.?"

"Mitch? Jake? Reece Jr.? *Those* are your picks? Those are totally boring," she counters.

"Those aren't boring, they're manly names."

"Oh brother," she mutters. "Why don't we just name him Axel or Zeus?"

By the time we pull into the driveway we're both laughing, and her basketball belly shakes like what I imagine Santa's would. Of course I'm not going to tell her that. I may be a guy, but I know better.

As we step into the house the hair on the back of my neck stands up. I grab Delilah, covering her mouth with my hand. "I need you to listen and do exactly as I say. Nod your head." She does slowly, but I don't miss her body trembling. "Baby, I want you to go get in my car. Lock yourself in, and if you hear anything that doesn't sound right, then just throw it in reverse and back right out of the garage. I don't care if you take the whole damn thing down—you just get out."

I kiss her lips hard, and then watch as she slips

out the door into the garage. I pull my gun out of my ankle holster and flip off the safety. I move throughout the house and look under any nook and cranny, but there's no one here. I flip the safety back on and open the garage door. I signal for her to come in.

"Are you sure it's safe?"

"Yeah, I went through the whole house, baby. There's no one here."

She disappears upstairs to change, and I pull out the burgers I'm grilling for dinner tomorrow night. When Delilah comes back down she's quiet, but still gives me that beautiful smile. The t-shirt she's wearing hugs her figure and shows off her baby bump. Her shorts are snug around her ass, and my dick's getting hard just looking at her.

I turn my back to her to adjust myself and check out the refrigerator. "Later do you want just a snack?" We ate a lot of pizza at Egan and Carrie's.

She takes a drink of her water, and again my dick twitches. What is wrong with me? I shake it off, and don't miss the underlying feeling that sours my gut. Maybe I'm just paranoid, but I'll just be extra watchful tonight.

Being with her is easy, effortless. I've worried that our age difference would be a problem, but it hasn't been. Maybe growing up the way she did, she had to mature a lot faster. I don't really understand how someone could treat their child the way Delilah's mom has treated her.

We settle on the sofa. I'm sitting down in the corner and Delilah is lying with her head in my lap while I watch the six o'clock news. My fingers absently sift through her hair, and it isn't long before her soft snores fill the living room.

It's safe to say I'm falling in love with her, and I know it's fast and things are complicated, but it feels right. Moving to Chicago was one of the best decisions I've ever made. It was a fresh start, and a chance to use my skills. Prior to Jack asking me to join his team, I'd thought about going into law enforcement, but this suits me a lot more—everything suits me better here.

I met Delilah; I've made good buddies, so I get that brotherhood I miss from my time in the service; I have a career; and now I'm going to be a father. All of these changes should scare me or stress me out. I've always liked having a routine, and having Delilah here took some getting used to. Babies change things too, but I've never backed away from a challenge.

I love the child already and he's not even here. My doorbell chimes, and she pushes herself up looking so cute and confused. "Let me get up, baby."

She gets up off the sofa and disappears upstairs, probably to go to the bathroom. I make my way toward the door. The voices on the other side cause my body to lock up. I should've expected this sooner. When I pull open the door, my mom launches herself at me. "Oh my handsome boy, I've missed you so much." My mom is an itty-bitty slip of a woman, and I'm still amazed that she was even able to carry me.

"I've missed you too, Mom." She squeezes me before letting go so I can greet my dad. "Hey, old man." He grabs me and pulls me into a back-slapping hug. I step back and look at both of my parents. They're both in their mid-fifties, but don't look it. My mom's always been trim, and her brown hair is free of gray, which I'm sure is thanks to hair coloring. My dad is in great shape, but leaner than me. His dark blond hair is more silver, but it works on him.

"We just had to come see how you're doing, and meet the mother of my future grandson," my dad says. They both turn toward the stairs, and I turn to find Delilah standing at the bottom of the stairs, holding her belly and looking nervous.

I hold my hand out to her, and she walks slowly toward us. "Baby, these are my parents, Elizabeth and Richard Meyers. Mom, Dad—this is Delilah Mackenzie."

She steps forward. "H-Hello. It's very nice to meet you both."

Mom reaches for her hand first. "Lovely to meet you." She looks at her stomach. "May I?" Delilah immediately agrees, and I watch my mom place both hands on her belly. I know he kicks and my mom feels it because she looks at me with a huge smile on her face. "He's strong just like his daddy."

My mom steps back and my dad shakes her hand, but doesn't touch Delilah's belly. We head into the living room and sit down. "How long are you guys going to be in town for?" I ask.

"Only a couple of days. We didn't want to intrude…too much." Mom winks at me, and Dad just shakes his head.

"You're welcome to stay here."

"No, on our way here your mom booked us a hotel room. Since we didn't tell you we were coming, we didn't want to assume that you didn't already have plans. We didn't want to get in your way."

My mom has never had a problem butting in on our lives—of course in the most loving, yet irritating way. I tell them about work and the guys I work with, including Delilah's dad. I don't really like the look that they both give her. It's a judgy look, and I know she's uncomfortable, but I'm an idiot and stay silent.

"Can I get you folks something to drink?" Delilah stands up and starts backing out of the room. My parents ask for water, and she escapes to the kitchen like her ass is on fire. I turn back to my parents and give them a pointed look. Delilah brings out the bottles of water. "I'm gonna head upstairs and give you a chance to catch up." She yawns and covers her mouth with the back of her hand. "It was nice meeting you folks."

"Good night, dear," my mom says.

"Nice meeting you, Delilah." Dad gives her a forced smile.

"Let's go sit on the back deck," I tell them. Of course I don't mention it's so I can chew them out for the way they treated her.

They follow me through the kitchen and out the sliding door. We sit at my table, and I look between the two of them. "Are you kidding me right now? You know I love you and respect you, but you made Delilah really uncomfortable. She's a sweet girl and doesn't deserve that."

My dad puts his hand up. "Son, you called her a sweet girl...*girl*, not *woman*. She looks like a teenager. You know what people will say when they see you together?"

"Seriously, you make it sound like she looks like she's twelve, and she's almost twenty-two. You could at least try and get to know her. You'd find out that she's sweet, smart, loving, and loyal. She's going to make a great fucking mom, even though she's got a shitty one. I'm happy, and isn't that what you want for me?"

"Honey, we love you, and we're glad you're happy, but is this really what you want? You're going to be in your forties, and she'll still be in her twenties. Honey, you can't possibly think this is a good idea. You work for her father. Do you think you'll still have a job if things go south with the two of you? Are you sure it's your baby?"

I'm surprised that they're treating me like I'm a dumb kid who doesn't know any better. "Are you guys kidding me right now? You come into my home, disrespect me, and the mother of my son. I know you care, and you think you're trying to help me, but I think I'm pretty good at reading people, and she's amazing. She didn't hesitate to let me be involved with my child. No games, no threats, and straight-up honesty is what I've gotten from her." I stand and look at two people I've respected and loved, and it feels like I'm looking at strangers.

"I love you. You know I do, but if you can't treat her with respect I can't have you coming around and upsetting her."

They both look at me, the regret easy to see.

SECURITY BREACH

"You're right, son. Your mom and I would like to take you out tomorrow night for dinner. Let us get to know her. We'll make it right."

"Yeah, honey. I'm sorry that we made her uncomfortable."

I stand up. "I'll be right back." Once inside, I head upstairs. It's extremely silent. In my room, I don't find her. I move to her room, and it's empty, but there's a piece of paper lying on her bed.

Reece,

They're right. I'm too young for you. I can't make you happy. I'm going to Brandon's. I'm sorry.

Love,
Delilah

Chapter Twelve

Delilah

My eyes burn as I pack my bag. How could I even be so naïve to think we'd ever work? He's older, worldlier, and obviously has his shit together. Me…I'm barely an adult, and got pregnant after a one-night stand.

I throw my bag over my shoulder and hurry down the stairs. The Uber I called pulls up in front of the house and on quick feet I head out to the car. I throw my bag in the backseat and climb in the front. The driver doesn't try to engage me in conversation…thank God. I pull out my phone.

Delilah: *Are you home?*

Brandon: *Yep, what's up?*

I blink rapidly, trying to stave off the tears.

Delilah: *I left him.*

SECURITY BREACH

Brandon: Oh fuck. Okay see you when you get here.

Twenty-five minutes later, the driver pulls up in front of my apartment. I grab my bag before thanking him and shutting the door. Brandon comes walking out and wraps his arms around me. He leads me inside and we head up to our apartment. He drops my bag by the door and leads me to the sofa.

The baby can tell I'm upset because he's moving around. I know I need to calm down. I blow out a deep breath and prop my feet up on the coffee table. Brandon sits down on top of it next to my feet and places them in his lap. I close my eyes and moan as he massages my constantly sore tootsies. "Tell me what happened."

I go over the whole mess, and it's then that I begin to cry. "They think I'm too young for him. They asked if he was sure this was his baby. I get it, I really do, but if I wasn't a million percent certain I wouldn't have told him. Plus, I hadn't been with anyone for a while before him. What am I gonna do?"

"Sweetie, I'm so sorry." He wraps me in his arms. "Go put your pajamas on, and we'll snuggle and watch *Top Chef*. After a good night's sleep, we'll talk."

I nod and stand up, grabbing my bag off the floor and carrying it into my room. I'm just brushing my hair out when I hear pounding on the door. My belly dips because I know who it is. I honestly don't want to see him right now, but I can't avoid him.

My bedroom door flies open, hard enough that it slams into the wall. I swallow hard, staring at him. His eyes are bright with anger. The apples of his cheeks are a slightly darker shade than the rest of his face.

"What the fuck were you thinking?" he growls out.

"Wh-What do you mean? I had to get out of there, Reece. I heard what they said, and you couldn't expect me to stay there when they clearly think I'm a child whore who chose you to be my baby daddy." Great, now I'm crying. I hate letting anyone see me cry. Brandon's the only one that I truly let see me lose it.

"If you would've fucking stayed, you would've heard me defending you, and them agreeing they were wrong."

I swipe angrily at the tears that are steadily sliding down my cheeks.

"I understand you're upset, but leaving was not smart."

"I couldn't stay and listen to it anymore, or have them stare at me like some loser that trapped you."

He paces back and forth like a caged animal. "Someone has been messing with you. Someone *hit you* in your belly. How fucking *stupid* could you be right now?"

It's like a movie on fast forward. Every mean thing my mom has ever said to me comes rushing back, hitting me like a ton of bricks. I stare at Reece while my heart breaks—his lips are moving but I don't hear what he's saying. How could I be so wrong about him? He's just like her, and it breaks my heart because I'm in love with him and have just been waiting for the right time to tell him.

He moves toward me, concern written on his face, but I begin shaking my head violently back and forth. "N-No! You need to go." Reece doesn't budge. "Leave!" I screech. "Go, I don't want to see you. I'm n-not st-stupid." Great, now I'm stuttering.

Why won't he leave? He stops right in front of me, but I can't hear what he's saying. Reece reaches for me, but I slap his hands away. Out of the corner of my eye, I see Brandon and Jose standing in the doorway. I look at Brandon, the only person other than my dad who has always been there for me. I thought Reece would be someone I could count on too.

Finally, it's like the volume is turned up, and I look up at Reece. "I'm sorry...I didn't mean that," he murmurs. "You *know* it's not safe for you here."

I suck in a lung full of air, straighten my spine, and look him in the eye. "I need you to leave. I don't want to see you. It may not be safe, but I'd r-rather take my chances here." I might as well let it all out while he's standing here. "I'm-I'm in l-love with y-you, and you've just broken my heart."

He grabs my face so fast it scares me, but all he does is kiss my lips hard. "I'll leave, but fuck me, I don't want to. This isn't over—*we're* not over. I'm falling in love with you, and I love our son. I'm not giving up on us, but I'll give you some space. I'm so sorry about what I said, but you have to forgive me for being stupid." Reece turns and walks out of my room, and I hear the front door open and shut.

Sinking onto my bed, I lie on my side and let the

tears flow. The bed decompresses before an arm wraps around my middle. "Del, it's going to be okay. I'm not taking his side, but he *did* look like he felt bad. He's not your mom, baby girl. He looked so worried when he got here."

"Today was just a really bad day," I say between sobs.

"Well lucky for you, tomorrow is a new one."

***

I walk into the office with my head down. Luckily, it's early and Shayla isn't here yet. She'd ask me if I was okay, and I'd only nod because if I spoke I'd start crying again.

I move through the doors and practically sprint to my office. I know I look like shit, but I didn't sleep much and when I did it was fitful.

The bags under my eyes have bags, and I didn't bother with makeup or doing my hair—or at least any more than putting it in a knot on top of my head. I open my office door, flip on the light, and freeze, but that's because on my desk is a brown paper bag and a bottle of orange juice.

When I open the bag, I smile because inside is a huge chocolate chip muffin, four strips of bacon, and some scrambled eggs. There's a note leaned against the juice.

Delilah,
I wanted to make sure you eat breakfast. Have a good day.

Love,

Reece

A small smile graces my lips, and I set the note in my purse. It lifts my spirits...a little, and I dig in.

Once I finish I throw away my trash and drink the last of my juice down. I pull out my phone and send him a quick text thanking him, but ignore my phone when it dings in response. I'm still upset, and yes, he didn't mean to say it, but he did, and it hurt to hear those words I've heard hurled from my mom.

Everyone must get the vibe to leave me alone because they do, and I'm grateful. At lunchtime Shayla calls me to the front desk. There's Chinese food waiting for me. I take it back to my office and see it's my favorite—shrimp fried rice and crab Rangoon. Before digging in, I go to the breakroom. I find Erik and Marcus are watching highlights on ESPN.

They both turn to look at me and give cautious smiles. "Hey, boys," I say before heading back to my office. My son has given me a ferocious appetite, and I eat every ounce of my food. My office phone rings. "Hello?"

"Hi, honey."

I smile at the sound of my dad's voice. "Hey, Dad. How's your trip?"

"It's good, honey. How are you feeling?"

"Good. I just finished eating lunch. Just working on payroll, and then probably heading home. I came in early today." I pop a piece of gum in my mouth.

"I should be home by Monday the latest. Did you

get the email so you can send the bill out?"

"Yep, and actually I've already sent it." A thought comes to me, and I take a deep breath. "Dad?"

"What is it, honey?"

"Do you regret having me? Or at least having me with Mom?" Why is this stuff all coming out now? Why do I feel so insecure about my dad wanting me? Maybe it's the pregnancy hormones.

"Baby girl, I want you to listen to me. To really hear what I'm saying. I love you more than life itself. I would die before I'd let anyone hurt you ever again. I wanted you from the moment that test came back positive. Yes, we were young, and yes, we got married because you were coming, but I did love your mother once—it just didn't work out. The only regrets I have are leaving you with her when I was deployed, and letting her use you as leverage to get what she wanted, but that's on me." He's quiet for a moment.

The tears are falling in earnest now. I've never cried like this because my mom hated to hear me cry. I suck in a breath. "Thank you. I'm sorry I'm all emotional. It's just been a bad couple of days."

"Well I wish I was there to see to my girl. When I get home, we'll plan to do something. How's my grandson?"

I rub my free hand over my belly. "He's getting bigger and bigger. I imagine I'm going to be running out of room eventually."

He chuckles into the phone. "Well I can't wait until he's finally here. I'll see you when I get back, okay?"

SECURITY BREACH

"Okay. I love you, Dad."

"I love you too, honey. You're going to be an amazing mom." We hang up, and I do feel better. These hormones are no joke and have my thoughts all over the place.

When I'm finished for the day Erik takes me home, and then tells me he's going to be outside keeping an eye on things until Brandon gets back. I don't have to ask who set that up because I know it was Reece.

Up at my apartment, there's a box leaning against my door. I don't know for sure if it's safe, but then I recognize the handwriting. It matches the same penmanship that Reece used on his note with my breakfast. I carry it inside and sit it on the counter. Carefully opening it, I smile when I look inside. A huge bag of Skittles, a bag of powdered donuts, and my favorite jalapeño flavored chips are inside.

At the bottom is something wrapped in tissue paper. I carefully open it, and I smile even wider. It's a black onesie, and in red lettering it says, **"Momma's boy, and proud of it."** I lift it up and lay it on my belly. It's so tiny, and I can't imagine my baby being that small.

I take everything into my room and set it on my bed. Why does this not feel like my room anymore? Last night I hadn't noticed it because I was upset, but now I feel like this isn't my place at all. I grab my phone and pull up Reece's number.

"Hey, baby."

"Thank you for the goodies, and the onesie. Thank you for breakfast and lunch today."

"I'm sorry about what I said. I was upset about my parents, and their behavior, and then I found you had left. I freaked out and took it out on you. You didn't deserve that, and knowing what your mom did, I should've known better. Please come home—it's not the same without you." The conviction is strong in his voice. I know he feels bad and didn't mean it.

I've never been one to hold a grudge. "Can you come get me?"

I hear a knock on the front door, so I run through the apartment and throw it open. I fling myself at him, or at least as much as I can with my big belly. He kicks the door shut and locks it without looking. With his lips on mine, he walks me backward until we reach my room, and I fall back on the bed.

Reece's tongue dances with mine, while he pulls my dress up from the bottom. His fingers slip into my panties, and I moan when he wastes no time shoving one, then two fingers inside of me. I moan again into his mouth as he tickles that spot deep inside me.

I grab his wrist to hold his fingers inside me as I begin to come embarrassingly fast. "Fuck, baby—you're squeezing my fingers so tight. God, I love the feel of your pussy." Once the tremors stop, he pulls his fingers from my spasming cunt. I moan as he licks my juices off each one. He kisses me, and I can taste my tangy flavor. I moan some more.

I've only ever tasted myself occasionally when I've masturbated. I didn't think I would like it, but strangely I do. Reece pulls away enough so he can stroke my cheek. "I'm so, so sorry."

I place my fingers on his lips. "It's okay. You didn't mean it."

"I know, but I should've known better. I can't guarantee that I won't say something stupid again because I *am* a man, and we say stupid shit. Come home with me, please?"

I nod, and he helps me up. "Wait, what about you?" My eyes go to the obvious erection in his jeans.

"We've got all night." He watches me as I gather my things, shoving them into my bag. Once that's all done, I send a quick text to Brandon.

Delilah: Hey B. Talked to Reece, going back to his place.

The three little dots begin bouncing.

Brandon: Good. I love you girl.

Delilah: Love you too. I'll call you tomorrow.

Hand in hand, we walk out to his car, and he helps me inside. We're both silent for the first few minutes of the drive, but he reaches out and grabs my hand. "I don't want you to be surprised, but my parents are at the house." He must feel my body stiffen. "No, they want to take us to dinner to apologize, and they also bought you a gift."

"They didn't need to do that."

"No, they didn't, but after you left yesterday, Mom felt bad that they didn't give you a chance."

We're quiet the rest of the way to his house. He

pulls in the driveway, and my pulse speeds up and my palms begin to sweat. I climb out, and he takes my bag in one hand, and my hand in the other.

His mom greets us at the door, and I don't miss her glassy eyes. "Delilah, I'm so glad you're back. I want to apologize for my judgmental behavior. You did not deserve that." She pulls me into a hug, and I immediately wrap my arms around her, or as much as I can with my belly in the way. "I am *so* sorry."

Despite every mean thing my mom has ever said to me, she's never apologized for any of it. This woman doesn't know me at all, but here she is obviously feeling bad. "It's okay. I know this is all a shock—"

She stops me. "Honey, you don't owe me any explanation. Come—I bought you a gift for the baby."

I follow her into the living room where Reece's dad is standing next to a bassinet with a big, blue bow on it. "Hi, darlin'."

"Hi," I say quietly as I move toward the bassinet. It has tan fabric with brown teddy bears all over it, and above it is a mobile with teddy bears hanging from it. "This is beautiful." I run my hand over it, and I know I'm smiling like a fool, but I don't care. There are two bags sitting in it; I grab the first and pull out several packages of onesies in newborn and one-to-three-month sizes. In the other bag are some sleepers. One is covered in baseballs and bats, and one has puppies on it.

I look at Reece's parents. "Thank you so much. This is wonderful."

"You're welcome, sweetheart. Are you guys

hungry?" his mom asks.

We ride with them as we head downtown to an Italian restaurant. His parents try very hard to include me in their conversations. Reece's mom shows me pictures of Rachel, his sister, and her kids. They're beautiful—they look like their mama. I show them pictures of Brandon and I, and my dad. I'm avoiding having to talk about my mom at all costs.

The whole night Reece is touching me, whether it's holding my hand, his hand on my thigh, or his arm around my shoulders. By the time his dad pays the check I have my head resting on his shoulder. I'm exhausted, both emotionally and physically.

They drop us off, and we go inside. I head up to get ready for bed because nine o'clock seems to be my bedtime now. After going through my nightly routine, I head downstairs and find Reece watching *SportsCenter*. I curl up next to him. I lean my head on his lap and he plays with the strands of my hair.

My eyes flutter closed, and then open, as I start to fall asleep. I'm not sure how much longer it is when I feel myself being lifted into the air, and then I'm moving. I open my eyes and see Reece is carrying me upstairs and into his room.

After laying me down, I hear clothes rustling and then the mattress compresses as he climbs into bed and pulls me snuggly against him. My eyes shut, and a sigh slips past my lips. How is it possible that I feel so connected to someone I just met a short time ago? I won't question it—I'll accept and embrace it.

Again, I've been unhappy or not as happy as I

could be for most of my life. I deserve to be happy now, and my son deserves it too.

***

This waddle that I've adopted this past week is comical. I feel like an Oompa Loompa, except for the fact that I'm not orange. I'm almost positive this baby has doubled in size the past two weeks. We've also started our birthing classes. I know Reece hates them, but he's a trooper and suffers through it.

I've decided I'm going to try hypnobirthing. It's deep relaxation, visualization, and self-hypnosis. It's to create a calm and serene experience. Of course, it'll help if I end up needing medical intervention.

Our class is small—it's us and four other couples. The instructor is okay, and I'd like her better if she didn't give Reece flirty grins and touches all the time. She always takes extra time to talk to him after class, totally ignoring that I'm with him.

I finish pinning my hair back and then head back into the bedroom. I slip on a long maxi dress and then a cardigan over it. Once I'm dressed, I sit down on the side of the bed. I'm freaking exhausted already. I have less than a month and a half to go, which I can't believe. It's hard to believe it's been a month and a half that Reece has been here.

I hear footsteps and find my man standing in the doorway. "You ready?"

I nod and stand up. When I reach him, I push up on my tiptoes and kiss his lips. "Sorry, I needed a minute after I got dressed. I'm so tired."

"Baby, stay home—your dad will understand."

"Reece, I'm pregnant, not sick. I'll be okay. It just takes a lot out of me getting dressed. Your son is a moose and sucking the life out of me." I head downstairs, packing up my laptop and the paperwork I brought home.

My phone rings and I grab it. "Hello?"

A sigh comes through the phone, and my stomach dips. "You still pregnant?"

"Yes, Mom, I'm still pregnant."

"I've sent you some brochures from a couple different adoption agencies. Look them over, and tell me which—"

I don't let her finish; I just hang up.

"Was that her?" I nod.

No tears fall. I'm resigned to the fact that she's never going to support me like a mother should. That's okay, though, because I've got a father who loves and supports me enough. "She's never going to accept this baby, and I'm finally okay with it," I say. "I wish things were different but they're not."

He wraps me in his arms. "That's not something you should have to get used to, or to deal with. If she calls again, you hand the phone to me, and when I'm done with her she won't be calling you again."

I smile up at him. "Thank you for that."

We make our way to the office a short while later, and when we step off I find my dad talking on his phone. He's pissed at whoever it is, but as soon as he sees me, he hangs up.

"Everything okay?" I ask.

He kisses the top of my head and then rubs my belly. "Yeah, honey. Just a business call. You look beautiful as always." He looks over my shoulder to Reece. "I need to meet with you this morning."

I don't like the sound of that. We all head to the back and get our days started.

Chapter Thirteen

Jack

As soon as Reece enters my office, I have him shut the door.

"What's up, Jack?" He sits down in the chair across from me. Did I want my daughter to be pregnant and single at twenty-one? No, but if I had to pick someone to be the father, it would definitely be Reece. He's a good guy and has taken really good care of Delilah.

This morning he sent me a quick text letting me know that the evil bitch called my daughter again. I'd called her and laid into her evil ass. I've offered her money countless times to leave my daughter alone, but she always tells me no because she loves pissing me off.

I hate that she's not a good mother to my girl. If I knew how she was going to turn out...well, I can't say that, because had I not been with Becky I wouldn't have Delilah, the best thing I've ever done.

"I wanted to let you know that I talked to Delilah's mom. I'm not sure it'll do any good, but I told her I'd give her fifty thousand dollars if she'd stay out of Delilah's life and stop telling her to abort her baby or put him up for adoption."

Reece leans forward and grounds out, "What…The…Fuck." He takes a deep breath. "Luckily Delilah has decided she's done with her, more or less. She knows her mom is never going to accept the baby. Jack, she's okay with it. I can tell she's hurt, but she's accepted it."

"But damn, that doesn't make me feel good. Her mother should be a part of this—teaching her about babies and guiding her through this. I've tried to be supportive, but I'm a guy, and fuck me, I was a kid when she was born. She deserved better parents."

"Jack, with all due respect your daughter loves you very much."

I sigh. "I know she does, and we've always had a close bond, but a girl needs her mother." Clearing my throat, I grab the file off my desk. "This guy is Becky's latest boy toy. His alibis check out for the time when Del was attacked outside of her apartment and when the rock went through your window. As much as Becky didn't turn out to be a good mom, she wouldn't stoop so low as to hurt her own daughter."

Just the thought of her being behind the shit with our daughter makes my stomach turn. I've felt her out over the phone, but I've gotten nothing.

"Is that where you were when you went on your business trip? Are you not telling Delilah that you've looked into her mom?"

SECURITY BREACH

I shake my head. "I can't tell her. I can't do that to her."

I only hope it doesn't blow up in my face.

Chapter Fourteen

Reece

I walk into the conference room, where my client waits to go over the proof I found that his wife is jumping ship and setting up a new life with her younger boyfriend. He's a nice guy and doesn't deserve the gold digger who's planning on taking their kids and half his money.

Our meeting goes better than I thought. She's a moron and didn't read the prenup; her infidelity is going to cause her to lose a lot. They'll share custody of the kids because he doesn't want them to be without their mom, and he's setting his soon-to-be ex in a fully furnished apartment with a monthly allowance.

He's a better man than me, because I don't think I would act the same way if my wife tried to pull some shit. When we finish talking, the guy seems to be okay. This isn't a fun part of my job—you always hope you don't find anything, but when you do, you're glad that they'll get the closure they need to get out of a toxic situation.

I walk him out and make him promise to call me if he needs anything. At the elevators, he shakes my hand and slaps me on the shoulder. "I appreciate your help, and your professionalism. I'll be in touch if I need you or your team for anything else."

"Thanks, Roger. You take care, and take care of those kids." The doors close, and I head to the back.

I make my way to Del's office to see if she wants to have lunch, but when I open her door I find her with her head on her desk. Her soft snores fill the space, and a warm feeling fills me. The pregnancy is taking a lot out of her, even though she tries to pretend that she's fine.

I close the door and then move around her desk to sit on top. She doesn't budge, even when I reach out and stroke my hand over her hair. I know most men want their sons to look like them, but what I wouldn't give to see her beautiful face on our son.

I grab her shoulder and give her a little shake. "Baby, wake up." It takes a few times before her eyes pop open, and her cheeks turn the most adorable shade of pink.

She sits up, and there's a wet spot from where she clearly drooled. Delilah wipes her mouth, and then looks around. "I only put my head down for a second...I swear."

I stand up and reach out to help her up. She groans as she stands up tall. I rub circles on her belly, and she rests her head against my chest. That seems to be her favorite spot to snuggle up to me. "Are you hungry?"

She looks up at me. "Starving."

"Can you go to lunch now?"

"Yep, I just need to use the bathroom first. I'll be right back." She disappears out of her office, and I step out into the hall to wait for her. The past week she's more tired than normal, like "fall asleep in the middle of a conversation" tired.

Delilah waddles back out a few minutes later. She gives me a sleepy smile that makes me nervous. I read that women can be tired at the end, but this seems a little extreme. I lead her out with a hand on the small of her back, and we ride the elevator down to the lobby. We walk around the corner to Fox's Bar and Grill.

We sit in the corner and order a couple of burgers. She smiles at me from across the table, and it's a sleepy, dopey-looking grin. "Are you *sure* you're okay? You look like you're fucked up."

She straightens her spine. "I'm fine, just tired. I *don't* look fucked up. How could you say that to me?"

I grab her hand from across the table. "I'm sorry, I didn't mean it like that. You just look…tipsy, and it's not bad, it's cute." I'm not going to tell her I'm worried.

After lunch, I practically have to carry her back to the office. The security guard in the lobby gives us a look. "Is she okay?"

"Yeah, she's just pregnant and tired." He nods in understanding. I lead her into the elevator and wrap my arms around her shoulders. "When we get upstairs, you're going to grab your things and go home, and get some sleep." She opens her mouth to argue, I'm sure, but I hold up my hand. "No arguing. You are dead on your feet. Maybe you're getting sick, and your body is trying to fight off something."

She doesn't say anything; she just leans her head against my shoulder and nods. As soon as we step off the elevator, I lead her to her office. "Gather your stuff, okay? I'm gonna let your dad know what's going on." I kiss her on the lips and leave her to it.

I find Jack in the breakroom getting a cup of coffee. "Hey, Jack?"

"What's up?"

"Delilah needs to go home. She's dead on her feet. I don't know if maybe she's getting sick or something."

Jack nods and then walks past me. I follow him into Delilah's office. As soon as I step inside, I know something is wrong. She's sitting at her desk, with her head resting on it. Her cheeks are flushed. Jack gets down next to her.

"Honey, what's wrong?" He places the back of his hand on her forehead. "You feel warm. I think we need to get you to a doctor."

I call her OB and she recommends taking her to her family physician or a walk-in clinic. Luckily, they're willing to fit her in. I promise her dad that I'll call as soon as I know something. She falls asleep in the car as we make our way to her doctor.

I wake her up and lead her inside. We check in, and since they're already seeing cases of influenza and summer isn't technically over yet, they make her wear a mask. I wrap my arm around her and feel it the moment she falls asleep on my shoulder. This is not normal, and she's been doing it a lot, but this past week it's gotten worse.

When it's finally her turn I follow as they take her into the back. They do all her vitals, and when they're done the nurse looks at us. "You've got a low-grade fever. It's a hundred and two. Just sit tight, and the doctor will be in."

The nurse shuts the door behind her, and I move to the examination table, helping Delilah lie down. I stroke my hand over her hair and watch her brown eyes flutter shut. The scent of cleanser burns my nostrils. Glancing around the room, it's got a calming feel to it. The walls are a soft yellow, and there are pictures of beautiful landscapes.

The doctor comes in a little while later, and poor Delilah has been swabbed, poked, and prodded. She takes it like a champ though, and by the time we're done she's diagnosed with fucking mono. He assures us that it's okay, and we'll just have to make sure we keep her fever under control and that she doesn't get dehydrated.

"Delilah, I'll want to see you again in two weeks." He looks to me. "If her fever isn't coming down with the Tylenol, or gets higher, you get her to the emergency room. No work until you come follow up with me. I'll send a report to your OB as well. Feel better and call if you have any questions."

After scheduling the follow-up visit, we head home. She turns to look at me in the car. "I can't believe I have mono. I've never been this tired—my body hurts so badly." She wraps her arms around herself. "I don't think I can miss two weeks of work."

"Babe, you can. You're contagious—what if you accidentally infect Egan and he takes it home to Leif and Carrie?"

She sighs. "Yeah okay, you're right." She grabs her phone out of her bag. "Hey, Dad—I have mono." A pause. "Yeah, he's taking me home now."

I really like that Delilah calls my place "home." She hangs up. "He said if I showed up he'd call security and have me escorted out."

A laugh slips from my lips. "Ha! Yeah, I can picture your dad doing that. When we get back to the house, let's look up what you can drink to keep you from getting dehydrated, and some foods that'll help you get better."

I pull in the driveway and go around the car to help Delilah out. After walking her upstairs to change into her lounge clothes, I make a list for the grocery store and text the guys to see if any of them are close and can come sit with her while I shop. Erik responds first and asks for the list, saying he'll grab the groceries.

It's very clear that the team all love and respect my girl. It's quiet upstairs, and I can guarantee she's already asleep. Sure enough, in our room I find her wrapped around the body pillow I bought her the other day. Her snores fill the room. I quickly change into some basketball shorts and a t-shirt.

Downstairs in the mudroom, I hop on the treadmill and start running. I'd rather be outside, but I can't leave her alone. By the time Erik shows up, my legs are wobbly, but I feel fucking great. I towel off, let Erik in, and help him grab the rest of the stuff.

"How the hell did Del get mono?" he asks with a laugh.

"Fuck if I know, but she's already passed out and snoring. I appreciate you getting this stuff." Erik follows me into the kitchen.

"Not a problem. Del's my girl—I love her like she was my own flesh and blood. What are you going to do during the day while you're working? I'm assuming you still aren't leaving her alone. Jack's got a case he was planning on giving us tomorrow that's going to keep us busy."

"I'm going to call my mom and see if she'll come, which I'm sure she will." I grab a beer for both of us. "Are you making any headway with Shayla?"

Shayla is giving him the cold shoulder. I'm actually surprised she hasn't quit yet, because Erik's always in her business.

"Nope, and just when I think she's letting me in, she does an about-face. Then I get the freeze out. I'm thinking I might as well cut my losses. Plus, why would I want to be tied down when I can get all the pussy I want?"

We sound like a couple of girls talking, but I don't believe him when he says he wants all the pussy. I'll be really surprised if he lets her go, and if he does, he'll be making a huge mistake.

My gaze drifts to the ceiling, knowing that the girl who undoubtedly owns my heart is sleeping right upstairs. What if I'd said no to Jack about the job after already sleeping with her? She'd be going through this alone, but prepared to do it that way.

That girl is an old soul, and more grown up than adults a lot older than her. Hell, just from the sound of things she's more mature than her mom.

I turn to the guy who, in the short time I've been here, has become like a brother to me. "If you say so."

"I do. I'm not going to keep chasing after a woman who clearly doesn't want me. It's whatever. We had a night of amazing sex, and connected more than I have with anyone."

I lean against the counter and cross my arms over my chest. "Maybe there's a reason she keeps pushing you away. She's probably had other relationships, and maybe she's gun shy. If Delilah kept pushing me away, I'd keep pushing back, especially if I could feel it down in my soul that we were meant to be together. I can't tell you what to do, but I will tell you this—if you give up, some other guy is going to snatch her up. Is that what you want—to watch her fall in love with someone else?"

"No," Erik grumbles. "Fuck, when did we turn into chicks, talking about our feelings and shit? I'll come by later this week to check on mono girl. See you at the office tomorrow."

He heads out, and I call my mom quick. She immediately agrees, and says she'll be there in the morning. Luckily my hometown is only three hours away. I wouldn't put it past my mom to be here by eight. She's a natural caretaker, and I know she wants to make it up to Delilah because of how their first meeting went. She's supposed to text me when she's on the road.

I grab my phone and call Jack. He answers right away. "How's my daughter?"

"She's sleeping, and I mean sleeping hard. I've got to wake her soon to give her some medicine for her fever, and get her to at least drink something." I grab the water with electrolytes out of the fridge and set it on the counter.

"What are we going to do about her safety? She can't come to the office, and I really need you with Erik on this new case."

"I know, I've talked to Erik already. My mom is coming in the morning to help take care of her. I'll go through the security system with her, and I figure if any of the guys are out running around, they could stop by and check on things." I hope he doesn't think I'm overstepping. I don't really know what Del and I are, but he's her dad.

"Fuck, thank you for handling things. I hate this is happening when there's some sick fuck messing with her. I'll set up a rotation with the boys and get in on it too. If you need anything from me let me know."

"I will." We hang up, and I start hunting for recipes to make for my girl. Google said to keep her away from breads and pasta—it can make her fatigue worse and cause inflammation. I grab the Tylenol and a bottle of water. In our bedroom, I find her in the same position as I left her. I lie down next to her and reach out, stroking her cheek.

Her lips are all smooshed, and she looks like my nieces would when they'd fall asleep on someone's shoulder. "Baby, wake up." I shake her shoulder a little, and nothing. "Del, wake up. You have to take medicine, baby."

She pushes up and looks around. Delilah has no fucking clue where she's at right now. "Was happening?" she slurs. "Why we here? I go sleep sleep." Delilah buries her face in her pillow and I chuckle.

"Baby, come on, you need to take these pills."

She lifts her head. "My throat hurts." All the laughter I felt moments ago disappears quickly.

"I know, baby—they said that could happen. Take these pills, they'll help you feel better." She lets me place the pills between her lips, and then drinks some of the water. "Good job. Do you need anything?"

She shakes her head and begins to cry. "I'm sorry I'm s-sick." I scoot back until I'm against my headboard, hugging her to my chest.

"Shh…baby, it's okay. You'll feel better soon, I promise. My mom's going to come and help out until you've got more strength, okay?"

"Okay." I help her stand up so she can go use the bathroom. I watch her walk out of the bedroom, but then jump out of bed because she bumps into the wall.

After helping her in the bathroom, I tuck her back in and she immediately falls asleep.

***

"Hey Mom, thanks for coming."

She cups my cheek. "Of course. Is she still sleeping?"

I nod. "Yeah, I got her up and force fed her

breakfast. She's taken Tylenol, and I made her drink a bottle of water. Her throat's starting to hurt, so one of the guys is going to bring throat lozenges and popsicles. Check her temperature in an hour, and make sure it stays low. She can't have ibuprofen—"

"Honey, I've been pregnant. I'll keep an eye on her, and maybe it'll be a good idea for her to come down here and lie down. I'll change your bedding, and maybe get her to change her clothes. Sometimes getting cleaned up does wonders. We'll be fine, and I'll call if there are any problems."

"I appreciate you dropping everything and coming."

"It's the least I could do."

I go over the alarm system and ask her to keep it armed at all times. She knows to ask to see IDs before opening the door to anyone. I've told her just enough for her to know to be watchful. She's a tough cookie, and my dad was adamant about her and my sister knowing how to protect themselves.

Upstairs I check on Delilah, and she's again wrapped around her body pillow. I lean down and kiss her forehead. "Bye, baby."

From her I get nothing. Her doctor said it could last a few weeks, or a couple months. I hope it's the former. This isn't the way she should be ending her pregnancy. Back downstairs, I kiss my mom's cheek and take off to work.

Chapter Fifteen

Delilah

Earlier I had been surprised to find Reece's mom here, but she's been amazingly sweet. She helped me downstairs and fed me this homemade vegetable soup that smelled so delicious I had two huge bowls. The baby liked it too, because it felt like he was doing a happy dance. Elizabeth was upstairs changing the sheets on our bed, and then she was wanting me to take a shower. She said I would feel better after taking one.

She made a little bed for me on the sofa to rest while she takes care of things upstairs, and I fight my eyes closing so hard, but an unknown time later I'm gently nudged until I look up into Reece's green eyes. I'm not sure why, but I began to cry. Maybe it's because the exhaustion that has taken over my body hurts.

It feels like my body is covered in teeny tiny pins. I know it's in my head, but every time I'm up I can't wait to go to sleep. Reece's large hand gently strokes my hair, and he whispers quietly in my ear. "It's okay, baby. Let it out. I wish I could take this from you."

He helps me upstairs, and then gets in the shower with me. It's totally nonsexual, but the intimacy makes me want to cry again. With a gentle touch, he washes and conditions my hair. I moan as he kneads my scalp.

After that he scrubs me from top to bottom. Paying extra attention to my belly, he places gentle kisses and talks quietly to it. I can't hear over the water, but I don't care because it's probably something sweet and amazing and I'll probably cry…again.

Once I'm rinsed off he helps me out, wraps a towel around his waist, and then gently towels me off. After getting dressed, he surprises me by blow drying my hair for me. Again, he does something so simple, but it means so much.

Since I slept so much earlier, he wants me to try and stay up to get some drinks in me. Downstairs, his mom is folding laundry at the table. "Dear, you look so refreshed. Do you feel better now that you've had a shower?"

"I do. Don't get me wrong—I'm still so tired and sore, but I don't feel grimy anymore." I check my temperature and it's 99.6. We decide to wait and see if it goes up.

I'm just ready to be done with this stupid infection.

***

SECURITY BREACH

It takes two-and-a-half weeks until I'm finally back to normal, or as normal as I can get being almost eight months pregnant. The past two and half weeks have solidified so many things; I wish Elizabeth had been my mother, or someone like her. Reece and his sister Rachel are very lucky, and I'm so green with envy.

She cooked for me, held me when I was so exhausted and tired of being tired. She was free with her affection, and never used it as a ploy to get my defenses down or give me a false sense of hope. By the age of ten, I'd already learned that hard lesson: be wary when mom wants a hug.

We Facetimed Rachel a couple of times, and I'm looking forward to meeting her, and soon. Because I'm contagious, or I was, we didn't think it was smart for her to come and possibly bring it back to her daughters. Speaking of daughters, hers are incredibly cute and look just like Rachel. Of course she looks just like Reece too, just feminine and beautiful. They all have dark hair and those mossy green eyes. Their skin has just a hint of an olive tone. They're going to be heartbreakers when they're older.

Second, Elizabeth had taken it upon herself to add some feminine touches to Reece's place, maybe to make me feel more at home. Pictures are now hanging up on the wall and lining the entertainment center. The ones on the wall are one of Reece and his Special Forces team, including my dad, who stood front and center; another is Rachel's family, and God, they're a pretty family; and the rest are more family photos, military photos, and then one that I can't stop myself from picking up and examining.

It was taken by his mom when they were here last time. We were at Luciano's Italian Bistro, and I'd worn a red, form-fitting dress that hugged the abundant curves I was carrying—especially in my breasts and ass, but I didn't care. The dress made me feel beautiful and not like a whale, which was how I felt most days. I'd worn my hair down in its natural wavy state. I kept my makeup light and wore a nude gloss on my lips.

Reece wore a blue button-down shirt open at the collar, black dress slacks that molded to his gorgeous ass, and black dress shoes. I remember posing for the picture, his arm wrapped around my waist, as his woodsy, spicy scent wrapped around me. I had my head resting on his shoulder, and my hand against his abs. We weren't looking at her—we were both glancing down because he'd made me laugh, and then *he* started to laugh. That's when the picture was taken.

Lastly, this whole mono situation just proved to me what an amazing man Reece is, and that he is going to be an amazing dad like mine is. Even when he was at work he'd call or text, checking on me and making sure I didn't need anything. Of course since I was asleep most of the time, this was conveyed by his mom.

Last week something happened, though. I'd woken up and come downstairs to see Reece, Elizabeth, my dad, and most of the team in the living room. They said they just wanted to come visit me, but I knew they were lying. The air had been supercharged, and they were all quick to say hello and then get me the hell out of there.

Trying to seduce the man you love into sex is no easy task when you were just sick, but I can't help it that the first thing to come roaring back is my damn libido. Last night in bed, I'd tried rubbing against his dick only for him to chuckle, kiss my forehead, and roll over.

I grab my laptop and set up my workstation—which is Reece's bed with a mountain of pillows that smell like fabric softener and make me sleepy immediately—but I shake it off because I have billing to do.

Luckily in my absence I was able to talk Shayla through sending me all of the info I needed to bill our clients. When Carrie comes back, I'm going to talk to my dad about keeping Shayla on. She can be our backup, and I'm sure I can find something for her to do—if not full time, then at least part time for now.

By the time Reece is home, I'm finally caught up. His mom brought me some soup earlier, but otherwise she left me alone so I could work. She goes home at the end of the week, and to be honest, I'm really going to miss her. Of course during these last few weeks she'd go home on Friday and come back Sunday night.

Anytime she does something sweet for me, I'm hit with a wave of sadness because this woman has cared more for me in the short time we've known each other than my own mother. I made the mistake of calling my mom last week to let her know I was sick, and she didn't answer or call me back.

I hate to say it, and it breaks my heart, but I'm done with her. As far as I'm concerned, my dad birthed me himself.

In the bathroom I brush my teeth and wash my face. I'm putting moisturizer on when Reece comes in. He was out in his mudroom, running on his treadmill. Now he's slick with sweat, and I want to lick him all over, but a yawn slips from my mouth. He steps behind me, wrapping his arm around my bulging waist. "Sleepy?"

Ugh…I don't want to admit that I am, in fact, exhausted. I nod solemnly, because this just sucks. He turns me around. "You're getting better every day." He kisses my nose. "Come on, let's get you to bed."

I pull away from him. "I don't want to go to bed. I'm tired of sleeping or lying down. I'm tired of being tired, and everyone treating me like I'm an invalid." I know I'm being irrational but I'm fucking tired of being tired. I want to get back to my normal routine.

"Hey, hey, hey, what brought this on?" He strokes a hand over my hair.

"Sorry, I'm just crabby. I'm okay." I lean my forehead against his chest, and sigh. The baby kicks me in the ribs, and I rub at the spot. "Your son has discovered my rib cage and is determined to get his foot jammed in there."

Reece places his hand on my belly and rubs the spot where our son's been kicking me. He grabs my hand. "Come with me."

I let him lead me into the bedroom, and he has me climb up on the bed. He climbs on and gets behind me. At the first contact of his fingers on my back, a moan rips from my lips. Reece's fingers are magical as they knead my shoulders and neck.

His touch is firm yet soft, and I'm putty in his hands. He doesn't say anything—he just works out every knot in my shoulders and loosens every stiff muscle from spending ninety percent of my day in bed. After he gets me all loose, he moves off the bed but settles me on the pile of pillows. Reece grabs my foot and begins kneading my instep. My eyes flutter shut and I moan.

It isn't long before I fall asleep.

***

Reece

The moment she falls asleep, her body goes loose. Her snores fill the room—I read in one of the pregnancy books that the snoring can sometimes get worse toward the end. Even though she's still a little pale and a little thinner than I'd like, she's still the most beautiful woman I've ever seen. I climb off the bed and head into the bathroom to shower.

After finishing, I throw on some gray cotton shorts and a plain white t-shirt. I find my mom curled up on the back deck, reading. She smiles as I sit down across from her. "Where's Delilah?"

"I massaged her shoulders, and then her feet. She fell asleep once I started on her feet. She seems to be doing a lot better these past couple of days."

Mom sets her book down. "She's been up most of the day, but if she overdoes it, she usually needs a nap. Her doctor the other day said he was happy to see she was doing better, and wasn't concerned about her weight loss. They're going to do another ultrasound at her next OB appointment." She shakes her head. "I hate that you're not going to tell her about the box."

Last week we'd been having a debriefing when my mom called me over and over until I answered. She was panicked, and I couldn't understand what she was saying. Jack had taken my phone, talked to her, and then called the team to meet at my place.

She was standing in the front door when we got there. I'll never forget the way she trembled when I hugged her to me. She had us all go into the mudroom where a box sat open. A part of me didn't want to look, but I knew I needed to see what was inside.

I stepped toward it, and when I peered inside I felt my body stiffen to the point that the air around the room felt wired. Inside the box was a baby doll with an ultrasound picture of my son attached…and a knife through it.

Mom said that it came by UPS and she only opened it because she thought maybe it was a gift or something Delilah ordered. We bagged it for prints, and Jack was going to take it to the station. Collectively, everyone thought it best not to tell Delilah. She didn't need the stress when she was already not doing well.

I look at my mom. "I know you think we should tell her, especially now that she's feeling better, but she's almost eight months pregnant. She doesn't need to be worried. If things escalate, *then* we'll tell her."

She lets out a huff. "I think you're making a big mistake. How can she keep her guard up if she doesn't know that things have escalated? I can't believe her father agrees too. At least she'll be back at work next week, and she'll be protected by lots of security. I guess it's a blessing that she's been sleeping so much she's missed the random drop-ins of your team." She starts laughing. "Erik is something else, and always stops by when it's time to eat. I swear that boy has a sixth sense when it comes to my cooking."

"Yeah, he says he's had to hit the gym extra hard." I lean forward. "I seriously can't thank you enough for dropping everything and coming to help with Del. I just started my job, and I'd already taken cases."

Mom grabs my hand. "I'm so happy to do it. I'm just sorry I was ever snooty toward her. She may be young, but she's an old soul. I've seen a change in you since you came here. After you left the service you seemed lost, you kept to yourself, and…I don't know, you seemed unsettled."

I can tell her eyes are getting bright with unshed tears, but she holds up her hand before I can talk. "Now you seem…happy. It feels like you're home. When I watch you with Delilah, I can tell how much you care for her. It's not just because of the baby, either. It's like you're two halves of a whole, and I'm so happy for you."

"Thanks, Mom. That means a lot."

Chapter Sixteen

Delilah

I stomp out of my OB's office with the dickhead Reece chuckling from behind me. Today I had my follow-up and ultrasound, and as of right now the baby is about eight-and-a-half pounds, and I still have a month to go. "I don't know how you can laugh right now. This is entirely your fault." I reach his car and stand next to it with my arms crossed over my chest in a huff.

He comes around and places his hands on my shoulder. "Come on baby, don't be mad."

"I'm going to have to push that thing out of my hoo-ha." I point to his crotch. "That thing is never coming near here again." I make a circular motion around my vaginal area. Reece throws his head back and barks out a laugh that I've never heard from him, and I love it.

He pulls me to him and kisses the top of my head. "I love you." Reece's voice is so quiet I barely hear it.

SECURITY BREACH

I tilt my head up and look into his eyes. "I love you." I push up on my toes and kiss his lips softly. He grips my hair at the base of my skull, taking over the power and intensity of the kiss. I moan into his mouth and feel that tingle begin between my legs.

It's been just about a month since I first got diagnosed with mono, and I feel great. Oh sure, I get tired quickly, and my hips hurt, but that's just part of being pregnant—apparently I'm pregnant with a monster baby. At least that's what it feels like on my smaller frame.

A horn honking in the distance has us pulling away from each other, but I don't miss the heated look in his eyes. I feel it all the way down to my pussy. He quickly helps me in, and as I buckle myself in, he climbs in and we're off.

The air is thick in the car as we head closer and closer to home. Once he pulls into the driveway, we both dash out of the car and into the house. I run as fast as I can up the stairs with him following close behind me.

We hit our room, and he has my dress up and off, and I pop the front hook of my bra. He turns me to face him, and I want to cover myself. My body has changed so much since he came back into my life. Hell, it's changed from the last time we had sex.

He grabs my face in both hands. "Don't hide from me. You're so beautiful growing our baby inside you." Our kiss is languid and deep. My tongue dances with his. He lets go of my face and cups my breasts; I moan as he pinches my nipples.

They're still so sensitive I could come right now.

I slide my hand down the front of his pants and feel his cock is hard. I give it a squeeze as he begins to kiss down my neck, but it's too hard for him to do right now, so he helps me climb on the bed. I scoot back and watch as he reveals his beautifully muscular body to me, and as always, my mouth waters at the sight of his thick cock.

He climbs onto the bed and moves toward me. Unfortunately, my belly gets in the way of him getting on top. Instead he lies next to me. Our legs tangle together as our mouths touch, and I sink into his kiss. "I've missed this," I whisper against his lips.

"Me too baby, me too." His hand moves between my legs, and I moan as he zeroes in right on my clit and begins to rub tiny circles around it. I'm embarrassed right now because I'm so wet, but his appreciative groan tells me I shouldn't be.

He moves his fingers to my entrance and pushes two inside. My channel grabs him, trying to pull his fingers in deeper. His lips travel down my neck, his teeth nipping at the skin along the way. My eyes slide shut as he wraps his lips around one nipple, pulling it deep into his hot mouth. I grip his hair as he works one nipple and then the other into his mouth. He nips the tip with his teeth. I cry out and arch my back as much as I can.

My orgasm comes over me so quick that it startles me. "Oh God!" He rubs that magical spot inside me, and I can feel the wetness that comes rushing out of me. I clamp his hand with my thighs as he slowly brings me back down. He kisses back up my chest until he reaches my lips.

He removes his fingers and brings them to his mouth. Reece's tongue comes out as he licks every drop of my cum from his fingers. He kisses me once before rolling me away from him on my side. He lifts my leg just enough and I feel him slide inside of me. I moan long and loud.

I welcome the burn and ache as he eases his hard cock into me. "Fuck, baby, you feel so good." He kisses my neck as he slowly moves in and out of me. Reece reaches down, holding my leg higher to pick up the pace, thrusting harder inside of me. "Del, you're going to make me come hard."

Turning my head, I wrap my arm around the back of his head, pulling him down to kiss me. I can still taste a little bit of myself on his lips, and I moan. He begins to grunt, and then groan. His thrusts become erratic, and the moment I feel his seed spilling inside of me, I begin to come again.

We ride the wave together until we're both panting for breath. "I needed that," I whisper.

Reece kisses my shoulder, pulls his softening cock out of me, and hugs me to his chest. A sigh slips past my lips, and I feel so content right now. The slight smell of sweat, laundry detergent, and Reece's woodsy scent wrap around me, and I snuggle further into him.

"Me too, baby. Are you getting hungry?"

I nod.

"Okay, let's get cleaned up and I'll take you out."

We both climb out of bed and I slip his t-shirt on over my head as I head into the Jack and Jill bathroom to get cleaned up. I brush out my hair, throw it up into a bun, and add a little makeup to my face.

I head back into our bedroom and throw on some black leggings and a white form-fitting t-shirt with a red quarter sleeve cardigan over it. Summer is coming to an end and nights are starting to become cooler. Reece comes back in from the en suite wearing his typical uniform t-shirt and jeans.

"You're so beautiful." He tips my face up and kisses my lips.

"Thank you, but I feel like a whale."

"You're not a whale, and soon we're going to have a little boy to snuggle and love."

"I wish we wouldn't have missed all those classes we signed up for when I was sick. I don't feel prepared at all."

"Babe, people had babies long before those classes. No one is ever ready, but we'll just learn as we go. Plus we've got his crib, dresser, a bassinet, some clothes, and don't forget my mom's been sending boxes every week full of goodies. We've got plenty of time."

We head out to the Mexican restaurant that I absolutely love called La Prima. After we get seated and order our drinks, I grab a chip and dip it into their homemade salsa. After eating it, I look up at Reece. "Your mom called today and she and Rachel want to throw us a baby shower, but after the baby is born so your family can all meet him."

Things were awkward between his parents and me at first, but I've learned to really care about them. They're good people, and just love their son.

SECURITY BREACH

Elizabeth has treated me better in the time I've known her than my own mother ever has. When my mom realized I wasn't going to be the party pal she wanted when I was in my teens, the teasing began. She wanted a friend, not a daughter.

"Are you okay with that? My family is kind of kooky."

I roll my eyes. "Please. Your family is great. I just can't wait to meet your sister face to face. She's got pictures that she's dying to share with me." I rub my hands together gleefully. "I bet they're good ones."

Reece shakes his head. "Leave it to Rach to pull out what I'm sure are embarrassing photos."

Our waitress comes to take our order, and I roll my eyes when she completely dismisses me and openly flirts with Reece. Of course, he's either ignoring it or totally oblivious because he can't take his eyes off of me. I never expected that the one time I gave in and had casual sex with someone would lead to a baby and falling in love.

After dinner, we decide to go see a movie. I hate that we're kind of limited with what we can do right now, but he always assures me that he isn't that big into going out in the first place. Of course it was a bar that we met at. He swears he was there just to eat and watch whatever game was on.

On the way to the theater, we decide to see a comedy. We grab drinks—water for him, lemonade for me—and he buys me a bag of Skittles and small popcorn. I feel like a pig because of course he doesn't want snacks, but with his body in the shape it is, apparently he doesn't have room for Skittles or popcorn.

Unfortunately I fall asleep about halfway through, only to wake up when the credits are rolling. "Oh my God. I fell asleep." I cover my face with my hands. "I'm the worst girlfriend ever." He freezes at my words and I realize what I said, which in reality is ridiculous because we've said "I love you" to each other. I peek at him through my fingers. "Am I your girlfriend?"

"Delilah, I love you, we live together, and we're having a baby. We're so much more than boyfriend and girlfriend."

"Is living with you temporary? I know before it was because of everything going on, but I don't want to assume you want me with you permanently. I still have a lot of stuff at Brandon's."

He places his hand on my belly. "Of course I want it to be permanent. Baby it's you, me, and little man. We really need to decide on a name, or at least have an idea."

I wrap my arms around him the best I can and hug him tight. "What about Jackson Reece Meyers? That way it's part of you and part of dad?"

"I thought you were going to give the baby the middle name Brandon."

"I know, but nothing goes with Brandon when it's the middle name. He'll understand, and…I could always use *his* middle name, which is Jeffrey." It's like a lightbulb flicks on. "What about Reece Jeffrey Meyers?"

"Let me think on it. I don't know how keen I am on the middle name Jeffrey. We can have lots of ideas and wait until we meet him to decide."

SECURITY BREACH

We head home, and my heart is full. I'm in love, I'm going to be a mommy soon, and even though they haven't found out who attacked me, life is pretty sweet right now.

Reece pulls down our street, and we both see the car that's parked in his driveway. "Do you know who that is?" I ask.

"No, I thought maybe you did."

Since whoever is here is blocking him from pulling into the garage, Reece pulls up to the curb. "Don't get out until I come around and get you." I do as he asks, and he opens the door for me. He keeps himself between me and the car.

The door of the other car opens, and Reece moves to block me from view. He reaches toward the back of his pants and I realize he's carrying a gun. His hand rests on the butt when I hear a voice I never expected to hear.

"Well, look at you. You're as big as a house." My mom steps around the hood and holds her arms out. "Come give me a hug."

Not wanting her to throw a fit I begin to move toward her, but Reece stops me with a hand around my waist. "Stay by me."

She moves toward us with a smile on her face that confuses me. It looks like she's actually happy to see me. Mom looks between the two of us, and her smile widens. "This must be the daddy. Hi, I'm Becky, her mom."

"I know who you are."

Mom's eyes narrow as she looks between the two of us. "Why won't you let me hug my daughter?"

"Maybe because up until a couple of months ago you asked her to get rid of our baby, and I'm not okay with that."

"Oh come on, it's not like she did it." She signals to my belly. "Delilah Renee Mackenzie, come give me a hug."

I look up at Reece. "It's okay." Placing my hand on his stomach, I smile up at him.

Reece leans down and presses his lips to mine before letting me go. I move toward my mom, and she opens her arms wide for me. I know I'm stupid for doing this—this is probably some ploy of hers, but when I reach her I let her wrap her arms around me in a tight hug. Mom pulls back but still holds onto me. "You look absolutely beautiful." She must notice my skeptical look. "What? You do. I'm just trying to be nice."

"You're right. I'm sorry, thank you. What are you doing here?"

"I hadn't heard from you, so I called Brandon and he said you were sick." My mom obviously didn't get my message.

"Mom, that was weeks ago." Of course she waited…why would *my mother* rush to make sure I'm okay? Meanwhile Elizabeth, Reece's mom, dropped everything to come and take care of me for three weeks.

"Well, you didn't expect me to come and possibly catch what you had, did you?" She looks between the two of us. "Are you going to invite me in?"

Reece grabs my hand and then looks back at my mom. "Come on." Mom follows us inside, and

SECURITY BREACH

Reece leads us into the living room. He turns to me. "Do you want some tea?"

"Yes, please. Thank you."

I don't miss my mom's eyes following him to the kitchen. She then turns back to me and gives me an overly sweet smile. "When is the baby due?"

"I've got about four weeks left. My actual due date is October sixth."

"I can only stay a couple of days because I don't have much vacation time. Plus I need to get back to Mitch, but while I'm here, I want to get some stuff for the baby. I'd also like to maybe take you to dinner, or at least make you dinner before I go."

Who is this person, and what has she done with my mother? Can I trust that her intentions are honorable? It's too soon to tell. "Umm...that would be great, but you don't cook."

She throws her head back and laughs. "You're so right. I'll take you out to dinner, then."

Reece comes back in with my tea and sits right next to me, wrapping his arm around my shoulders. Awkward silence fills the room as Reece stares at my mom with assessing eyes, and my mom scopes out the living room.

"Where are you staying tonight?" I know what she's going to say, and I'm worried about how Reece is going to react.

"I thought I could just stay here with the two of you. Is that okay? I drove all this way."

Reece stiffens next to me. I take a sip of my tea and look up at Reece with pleading eyes, because what if she really *is* trying to be supportive? What if she really *wants* to be a part of her grandson's life?

"You're welcome to stay here." Reece sounds like he's in pain just saying the words. "But if you say anything that will upset her, I won't have any problem putting you out. Do you understand me?"

Mom doesn't hesitate. "Of course I understand. What kind of person do you think I am?"

I can feel the irritation coming off Reece; placing my hand on his back and rubbing it seems to calm him enough to relax a little. I turn back to my mom. "Why don't you grab your bag and bring it in. I'll show you to your room."

"Thank you, honey. I'll be right back." We both watch my mom as she gets up to head outside.

Reece turns to me. "I don't like that she's here, and I don't trust her." He grabs my face in his hands. "I need to tell your dad that she's here. Promise me that you will be careful, and don't get your hopes up. I don't want to see you get hurt."

"I know. I promise I won't."

My mom interrupts us by coming back inside with a gym bag over her shoulder. Reece excuses himself, claiming that he has work to do, but I know he's probably calling my dad. He may not come over tonight, but I can guarantee that he'll be here bright and early tomorrow to assess the situation.

"Come with me and I'll show you your room." She follows me up the stairs and I lead her into the bedroom I slept in when I first got here.

"This is nice," she tells me as she sets her bag on the bed. "I appreciate you letting me stay here. Especially since I just showed up, but I wanted to surprise you."

I sit down on the bed, and she sits down next to

SECURITY BREACH

me. "I'm glad you're here." That's only partly true. Not until I know for sure she's not just trying to get money from my dad, or Reece if she suspects he's got money. Honestly, I don't even know if he does. We haven't really talked about it. I'm sure my dad pays me more than most office managers get, but I don't dare say anything because he'd get pissy. He says he pays me what I'm worth.

"Tomorrow we'll spend the day together. How does that sound? Just us two girls." She grabs my hand, surprising me.

"That sounds really great."

We talk for little bit longer before I leave her to get ready for bed, and head down the hall to our room. Reece is lying in bed looking at his phone. "Is she all settled?" he asks as I climb into bed.

"Yeah. Thank you again. I know the things I've told you paint her as a bad mom, but maybe she's ready to start trying."

"Promise me that you'll be careful, I'm serious—I know I said it before, but I'd feel better if you didn't get your hopes up," he says quietly before kissing my lips. We sink into bed, my back snug against his chest. "I love you."

I love to hear him say that. "I love you too." He touches me behind my ear, and his hand cups my belly.

Chapter Seventeen

Reece

After texting Jack right before bed the night before, I'm not surprised he shows up first thing this morning. I let him in and get him a cup of coffee before we head out to the back deck. He paces back and forth before stopping in front of me. "What the fuck is she doing here?" Both Del and her mom are upstairs getting ready.

"She claims she's here to spend time with Del. She'd called Brandon and he told her about Delilah being sick, so she waited two weeks before she decided to show up. She's taking Delilah shopping today for the baby." I look through the sliding doors, and then turn back to Jack. "I don't trust her, and I don't like it, but fuck, she seemed so happy her mom wanted to do something with her."

Jack scrubs a hand over his salt-and-pepper hair. "That woman is manipulative and doesn't stop until she gets what she wants. I swear to God if she hurts my little girl, I will make her pay."

"Do you think she's going to try something?"

"No…maybe…I don't know, but I've seen that woman let my daughter down over and over again." He moves closer. "For a split second I seriously thought she was behind the stuff with Del, but that idiot I told you she's dating had an alibi, so that's shot. By the way, the fingerprints on the box with the doll in it were just your mom's. Whoever sent it was fucking smart and probably wore gloves."

We don't talk longer because Del and her mom step outside. "Looking good, Jack," Becky says.

"Thanks, Becky. You've…had some work done."

I try not to snicker.

I don't miss the way that Delilah stiffens. I grab her and pull her into my arms, waiting for the fight to start, but instead Becky smiles widely. "Yep, and it was worth every penny. It was on your dime too." She reaches up and pats Jack's cheek, and I swear he looks like he's ready to pummel her, but Delilah puts her hand on her mother's arm.

"Mom, stop—please. Daddy, I'll see you later."

Delilah stops in front of me and pushes up to kiss my lips. "Mom's taking us to dinner, don't forget."

I watch her and Becky leave and let out a deep breath. "Jesus, is it like that always between you two?"

"Unfortunately, and I've tried being cordial for Delilah's sake. But I know how nasty that bitch can be. She's up to something, I can just feel it. Do we have someone on them?"

"Yep, Erik's tailing them all day. He'll make sure Delilah's safe."

Jack nods, and we head inside.

***

While Delilah is out with her mom, Jack helps me turn my office into the nursery for the baby. Right now the crib and everything is in the room that Delilah had been staying in; eventually my office will go somewhere else. I just hope Del loves what we're doing.

We're painting the walls a light gray color with robin's egg blue accents, or whatever the fuck it's called. My mom bought tons of stuff that Del doesn't even know about yet, her and Rachel both. The nursery is going to be completely decorated by the time Del gets home, and our son's dresser is full of clothes. A little bathtub sits inside the crib filled with baby wash, lotion, and powder. I'll never be able to thank my mom and sister for what they've done. They've made my girl feel like part of the family.

It takes most of the morning to paint, and Jack's been running a fan to help it dry more quickly. He doesn't want Del inhaling those fumes.

Erik texts me multiple updates, and it actually sounds like Delilah and her mom are having a good time. They hit the mall, Target, and stopped for lunch. This is exactly what my girl needed, and I hope her mom doing this stuff is because she genuinely wants to be in her grandson's life. Del is so strong, but I don't know if she could handle it if this was just some ploy.

We finish, and he slaps me on the back. "My

SECURITY BREACH

daughter is going to love this." Jack looks at me. "Please thank your mom and sister for me. I appreciate it so much."

Everything is moved into position, but the furniture isn't against the wall until at least tomorrow. We want to make sure the paint is dry. It's perfect timing too, because Erik just texted me that Del and her mom are heading back this way. Jack decides to leave, not wanting to see Becky again. I can't say that I blame him.

I jump in the shower and am just getting dressed when I hear the front door open. I slip into my boots before heading downstairs. The two women—who look more like sisters than mother/daughter—are carrying several bags in.

"Hey, honey." Delilah wraps her arms around my middle and tilts her head back for my kiss.

"What do you have in all these bags?"

"We got some sleepers and onesies. We got diapers, and I bought a breast pump for when I go back to work."

"That's great. Why don't you come upstairs with me—I want to show you something." I cover her eyes and lead her upstairs. I feel her mom behind me but I don't care. Nothing this woman does will make me forget the stuff I've heard.

Once we're up the stairs, I lead her to the door of the nursery. "Your dad and I wanted to do something special for you. Your mom taking you out today was the perfect distraction so we could do it."

I push open the door and remove my hand from her eyes. She steps into the room and slowly spins around. I begin to get nervous when she doesn't say anything, but she comes to stand right in front of me. "I love it so much. Thank you." Tears leak from her eyes, and I brush them away. "He's going to love sleeping in this room."

"I'm so glad you love it, baby. Once he's here and we pick a name, we're going to have it stenciled on the wall above his crib." She moves toward the dresser, picking up the frame, and I know what she's seeing—it was taken when my parents came to town. I had taken the selfie of us, and I was kissing her cheek while she smiled at the camera.

"I love this picture of us," she tells me.

"Me too."

Her mom and I head downstairs while Delilah takes a shower. I decided earlier that I'd just make us dinner instead of her taking us out. All I care about, though, is the fact that she's leaving in the morning. She's got me on edge, and I've had to pretend that I'm okay with the vile woman being here near Delilah and my son.

I pull the chicken out of the refrigerator and season it before setting it aside. Chopping up the vegetables, I ignore the fact that her mom is leaning against the counter watching me. I make the foil packets for the grill and set those aside before heading out to start it.

When I come inside, Becky is right where I left her, except she's got a twinkle in her eye that I don't like.

She moves until we're practically touching. "She sure picked a good one. You're so fucking sexy. I think you and I could have a lot of fun together…a *lot* more fun than that prudish daughter of mine. All her little boyfriends used to love to come over and have fun." Becky grabs onto my forearm. "I used to let them fuck me since Delilah wouldn't give it up."

Acid festers in my gut. This woman is fucking sick in the head. She's like the villains in those Lifetime movies my mom used to watch. "Do you hear yourself right now? That is your daughter, and I'm the man in love with her, and soon to be father of your grandchild."

"Oh, please. You don't have any idea how it was raising her. She always thought she was better than me, smarter than me, and prettier than me, but I showed her over and over again when the boys would come sniffing around. They'd take one look at me and forget *all* about her." I don't know if she wants me to be impressed by that, but all I feel is grossed out and disturbed.

I grab her hand and pull it off me. "Why are you doing this? What was the point coming here? You made her believe you wanted to be a part of her life, buying all that stuff for the baby."

She throws her head back and laughs. It even *sounds* evil, like some bad soap opera. "I wanted to see for myself what was going on between the two of you. You would've told me to get lost right away if I didn't seem genuine. Ugh…the whole time she talked about you, being in love, and that fucking baby. It was so boring, I felt myself almost fall asleep. The only fun part about her used to be Brandon."

Becky moves so fast I don't have a chance to

stop her. She grabs my dick and wraps her other arm around my neck, pulling me down and putting her lips on mine. I grab her shoulders and roughly push her back. "What the fuck? Why the fuck would you do that?"

I'm going to fucking vomit. I can taste her gum in my mouth. She smiles and then shrugs her shoulders.

"Get...*Out*!" I turn and find Delilah in the doorway. Her eyes are so fucking sad my heart breaks for her.

"Oh honey, I was just testing him. You don't want to be with someone who'll fuck your mom, do you?"

"All I ever wanted was for you to love me, but I guess that was too much to ask for. Get your shit, get the fuck out, and don't ever show your face around here again."

Her mom moves toward her, but I get in between them. "Don't look at her. Don't talk to her. Get your shit and go."

Becky smiles up at me. "She'll forgive me—she always does. Baby girl, you know I love you."

"You sure have a great way of showing it. I'm done with you. If anyone asks about my mom, I'm telling them that you're dead." I watch my girl bolt upstairs as fast as she can, and then hear the slam of a door—our door. "Becky, get your shit and leave now. If you don't, I'll send Jack to escort you out, because I bet he'd love to."

That crazy bitch sashays her ass up the stairs and returns ten minutes later with her bag. "I'm sure I'll be seeing you again," she says as she walks by me and out of the house. I move to the door and as soon as she pulls out of the driveway I lock it, run out to shut off the grill, and throw the food into the refrigerator.

I take the steps two at a time, and when I reach our door, it's locked. I put my ear to it and can hear her crying. "Baby, she's gone. Let me in, please."

She doesn't respond, and her cries become harder and harder. Delilah is killing me, and there's nothing I can do about it. "I know you're hurting right now, but let me in. Let me see to you."

I put my back to the wall and slide down until my butt is on the floor. "I'll be right outside when you're ready for me," I say to the door, hoping she can hear me.

I pull my phone out of my pocket and shoot Jack a text.

Reece: Hey Jack sorry to be the one to tell you but Becky came on to me tonight, said some hurtful things, and then left. Delilah's locked in our room crying.

Jack: That fucking bitch! I knew it, I knew she couldn't change. I'm on my way.

Reece: No, I'll text you when she comes out. I'm right here if she needs me.

The little black dots bounce before Jack responds.

Jack: Thanks for looking after my girl.

Reece: *Of course. I'd do everything in my power to erase that whole situation from her mind.*

I must've dozed off for a bit because the hallway is hidden more in the shadows. I hear a strange moaning sound from our bedroom. "Del baby, are you okay?

She cries, but I can hear her moving around in there. Her moan sifts through the door and it doesn't sound good. "Baby, open the fucking door. What's wrong?" Del continues to moan, and then cry.

I grab onto the doorknob and hit the door hard enough with my shoulder that it pops open. In the darkness of my room, I find her on the floor in the opening of the en suite. Rushing to her side, I drop down to my knees. "Delilah, what's wrong?"

She looks up at me, and her eyes are rimmed in red as tears continuously leak from them. "I-I'm h-having c-c-contractions." Her moan breaks my heart and scares the shit out of me.

I scoop her up into my arms and carry her down the stairs. I set her down while I grab my keys and wallet, and her purse. On the way to the hospital, I call her OB's answering service and ask them to inform the doctor that she's heading to the hospital.

When we get there, the valet helps Del out and into a wheelchair. I hand him the keys, and then I wheel her to the information desk. They send us to their labor and delivery unit and put us in a room. After she changes into the hospital gown, she climbs onto the bed so the nurse can monitor the contractions. Before she leaves us, she tells Delilah that she'll be watching from the monitors in the nurse's station.

Delilah stares at the wall, looking so sad. I pull up the chair and sit down next to the bed, reaching out to take her hand in mine. She doesn't squeeze it or hold on. It just sits limply in mine.

"Baby, please look at me." She turns to me and her brown eyes that usually shine so bright are dull and vacant. "I'm sorry, baby. I hate this so much for you. I wish I would've sent her away the minute she showed up."

A lone tear leaks from her eye. I reach for it and wipe it away with my thumb. A knock on the door sounds, and I turn my head to see Jack walk in. He takes one look at Delilah and opens his mouth, but I stop him. I get up and herd him out the door. "I want to see my daughter."

"You will, but man, I've got to tell you she is not doing well."

"What do you mean?"

"I think she witnessed everything that went down with her mom. That woman is a piece of work. She let me know that she fucked all of Del's boyfriends because Del chose to remain a virgin. She grabbed my dick and fucking *kissed* me. The smell of her perfume is still stuck in my nose, I can still taste her in my mouth, and I'm fucking nauseous. She thought we could have a real good time together."

Before I can say more, Jack grabs his phone out of his pocket, punches a few buttons, and holds it to his ear. "Just when I can't think you can sink any lower, you surprise me. Fuck me, Rebecca!" Oh shit. "I know you hate me, but that's our fucking *daughter*! Don't *ever* contact her again, and you will *never* get another dime from me." He hits a button and stuffs the phone into his pocket. "Take me to my girl."

Back in the room, Delilah is holding her belly and moaning. "Are you having another one?" She nods, so at least she's answering me now.

Her dad stands on the other side of the bed and grabs Delilah's hand. "Hey, baby girl. Is my grandson giving you trouble already?" She nods. I look at the monitor and back at her; her eyes are closed now. Jack sits on the side of the bed. "Del, don't let her get to you. She's not a good person, and that doesn't reflect on you. You are *not* her."

Jack sighs, moving into a chair on his side, and we quietly watch some college football. After about an hour, the nurse comes in. "Delilah, the doctor wants me to check you, and as long as you're not dilating, then you can go."

Jack excuses himself, and I grab Del's hand. The nurse slips on some gloves, squirts some gel on her fingers, and reaches between Del's legs. "No change from when you got here, but your cervix is definitely softening."

"Does that mean she can go into labor anytime? She still has a little over a month to go." I bend down, kissing Delilah's forehead.

"No, it can happen long before labor actually starts. What you felt today was called Braxton-Hicks contractions. Sometimes they can be simple tightening of your belly, sometimes they can feel like the real deal. If you feel them again, I want you to drink some water and lie on your left side. That'll usually stop them or slow them down. Go ahead and get dressed, and I'll get your discharge papers."

The nurse steps out, and I help Delilah get dressed. Her dad comes back in with the nurse and watches quietly as I lift my girl off the bed and into the waiting wheelchair. An aide comes and pushes her down to the lobby while I run out and give the valet my ticket. The aide wheels her out when my car arrives, and I get her settled inside.

Jack says he's following us to my place. She's silent the whole drive back, and just staring out the window. "Are you hungry? We never ate dinner."

She says nothing and continues to stare out the window until we arrive. After I help her inside, she goes upstairs, and I wait for her dad to pull in the driveway. I hold the door for him. "Did she go upstairs?"

"Yeah, I'm going to go check on her, and then I'll start the grill. I've got some chicken and vegetables in the refrigerator."

"I'll start dinner—you just see if you can get my daughter down here to eat." I slap him on the shoulder before heading upstairs. Taking the steps two at a time, I head up to my bedroom, but find it empty. I check the spare bedroom that her mom had slept in, but it's empty too. I open the door to the nursery and the strong scent of paint hits me, but what else I find obliterates me.

Delilah is sitting in the middle of the floor with a teddy bear in her lap. I sit down behind her, fitting my chest to her back. I wrap my arms around her, and I feel her body start to shake and know she's crying. I kiss her behind her ear. "I know. Fuck, I'm so sorry."

She turns slightly between my legs and buries her face in my neck. I hold her until her tears finally stop.

"Food's on," I hear Jack yell up the stairs.

"Will you eat something for me?" I ask her.

She nods. "Y-Yeah. I'm hungry."

Her voice is hoarse, and I'm sure she's got to be thirsty. "Come on, let's go eat dinner with your dad."

I lead her downstairs and she walks right into her dad's open arms. I give them a minute and walk into the kitchen to get plates and silverware out. They join me a few minutes later. Delilah is quiet during dinner, but she's eating and that makes me happy.

After we eat, she kisses both her dad and me and heads up to bed.

"Walk me out," Jack says, and I follow him. "Take tomorrow off. I don't want her coming into the office. She's too raw right now. It's taking all of my willpower not to go after that crazy bitch for hurting our daughter like that. I should've taken Delilah and run. I hate that she had to be raised by that cunt."

"You couldn't know that she was going to turn out like that."

"In the beginning I was blinded by pussy, and what I thought love was, but I knew nothing about love until they placed my daughter in my arms. Just wait—I know the love you have for Delilah is real, but as soon as you hold your son, you'll wonder how you ever lived your life without him."

I let Jack know that I'll update him on how our girl is doing tomorrow. He gets in his truck and I watch him drive away.

Chapter Eighteen

Delilah

I'm finishing up some invoices when thoughts of this past week hit me. It's hard to believe it's been a week since my mom showed up and tried to wreak havoc, and maybe she did a little, but that night I came to the conclusion that I didn't need her in my life anymore. I have my dad, Brandon, Elizabeth, and best of all, Reece.

Elizabeth called me the next day to check on me, after hearing about my mom, and when I started to cry she gave me the best pep talk. She told me that being a parent was the hardest, yet most rewarding job she'd ever had, and as sad as she found it, some women weren't cut out for motherhood. She told me that she saw the love I have for my son every time I put my hand on my belly already, and she didn't doubt for a second that I was going to be the best mother.

She promised to come see me next week, plus she wanted to see the nursery. Rachel is going to come with her too, which I'm super psyched for.

My dad's looking forward to meeting them. It felt like everything was falling into place. I've gotten a couple of hang-up calls the past week, but the number was blocked. I've tried not to let it bother me and live in fear, but I still remember the way it felt when the man hit me in the stomach.

The guys are still working their asses off trying to find the person who hurt me, but they're stumped and hitting dead end after dead end, which has pissed off the alpha brigade. They don't like to lose.

When I told Brandon about what happened with my mom, he'd felt terrible for letting it slip that I had been sick. I assured him that she was bound to show up anyway, and at least I knew the truth, and that was she didn't love me and didn't love her grandson. The only thing she loved was herself, and maybe whatever guy she was fucking, but that was only until they served their purpose and she scraped them off.

It still hurts, and every day I wake up with a heavy heart, but then I remind myself of what I do have. I have a father who'd do anything for me and loves me unconditionally. I've got a group of men that is doing what they can to keep me protected. They think I don't notice that someone's always tailing me, but my father *is* Jack Mackenzie. They should know better. They're always keeping watch.

Brandon is someone I can always count on and has been there for me always. Then there's Reece, and everyone that comes with him. They've shown me love and compassion, and they barely know me.

I focus back on my task, double-checking my

work before sending the bills out, and then I shut my computer off. I grab the gift bag from under my desk and carry it down to the surveillance room. I knock and wait for Egan to tell me to come in. Sometimes they're working on stuff that I don't need to see—that I shouldn't see.

"Hey, Egan," I greet him as I step inside, then sit down next to him.

"Hey sweetheart, how are you doing?" He leans over and gives me a quick hug.

"Good, just ready to meet this little booger. I was at the mall the other day and thought this would be cute for Leif." I hand him the bag, and he pulls out the little green sleeper that says, "Baby Hacker."

"This is fucking excellent. I can't wait to put this on him. Carrie's going to crack up."

I haven't been able to see Carrie and Leif because I've been sick, and then there was the stuff with my mom. "How are Carrie and Leif?"

"They're great. He's starting to hold his head up a little better. He's still an adorable bobblehead, though."

"I want to see them, but I've been trying to get caught up since I was sick. I've talked to her on the phone, but I know that's not the same as a face-to-face visit. Plus I need baby snuggles."

He gives me a smile. "I think she'd love that, and he already is quite the ladies man."

"I'm sure he is," I say with a laugh. "I'm finished for the day, so I'm going to get my stuff ready. Reece should be here soon to get me."

I stand up, but he stops me with a hand on my arm. "I'm really happy for you and Reece. I know everyone was worried about you when we first found out, but I see good things in the future for you guys."

"Thank you. I'll see you later."

I head back to my desk and find my man sitting in a chair across from it. "Hey, babe," I say and then bend down, giving him a kiss. "I'll be ready in just a second."

"No rush. Are you almost caught up? You've been working too much this week." He worries all the time about me.

"I'm about as caught up as I can be before this little boy comes." Reece rubs my belly and then leans forward, placing his lips on it. Our son gives him a big kick, and then he wiggles his butt, or at least that's what it feels like.

Reece leans closer. "Son, you quit kicking your mommy. You're getting too big to be doing that." He gives another kick, and we both smile. Reece looks up at me. "Get your stuff together, and when we get home I'll rub your feet."

That sounds heavenly because my ankles and feet are starting to swell a little bit. They're pretty sore by the time I get home. My ballet flats are about the only shoes I can wear right now. I grab my bag, and Reece takes it from me while I put my cardigan on.

Hand in hand we walk out, and I tell Shayla that I'll get ahold of her about doing lunch. That girl is full of secrets, and I'm looking forward to learning more about her. Hopefully she'll feel comfortable enough to share them with me if she chooses to. All I know is that I really like her and can totally see us becoming great friends.

"I look forward to it," she says and gives us a wave as we step onto the elevator.

When we reach the parking garage I scan it for his car, but I don't see it anywhere. "Um...where's the Shelby?"

"I put it in storage."

I stop walking and look up at him. "In storage?"

"Yeah, it dawned on me the other day that we're going to need something better to get a car seat in and out of. Also, something safer for when we're driving around with him in the car, and I couldn't do the minivan, so I got this..." He leads me to a sweet looking Toyota 4Runner. It's black, of course. These men all have a thing for black rides. He holds his key fob up and unlocks the SUV.

He helps me inside, and the interior is sick. The smell of new leather mixed with new car smell hits my nose. The leather feels soft and the seat is comfortable as I get situated in it.

When he climbs in, he turns it on and what looks like a mini computer screen lights up. "You just need to pair your phone, and you'll be able to use the hands-free. I'll go over everything else with you later."

"This is so sweet, but I don't know if I'll be able to handle driving something so big." As soon as I say it, I notice the innuendo and my cheeks flare up.

Reece chuckles and I turn and slap his arm. "Oh, you're pretty amazing at handling *big* stuff."

"I can't believe I said that." I stare at the ceiling and notice the sunroof. "You'll just have to help me learn how to manage something so big." I give him what I hope is a saucy wink.

He gives me a grin that makes my heart race. Pulling me toward him, he kisses my lips hard. I open to him as our tongues dance, and I fill myself get wet. He barely touches me and my body lights up. The kiss ends all too soon, and Reece pulls back. "After this baby is born, we're breaking in the SUV and I'm fucking you in the back."

My nipples harden immediately. When I look down, I see a tiny wet spot on the front of my shirt. I knew this would happen, but still it's pretty crazy that my body knows to start preparing for the baby's arrival.

Reece looks down and notices too. "Is that what I think that is?"

I nod. "Yeah. I guess I better start using those pads that your mom got for me."

When we reach the house, he pulls into the garage and I climb out. Reece carries my bag inside for me and sets it on the kitchen island. I head upstairs to change out of my work clothes and tie my hair up. I stop in the nursery and notice that Reece moved the furniture so it's against the wall now that the paint's dry.

I run my hand across the smooth wood of the crib and can already picture my boy snoozing away in here. Of course, for at least the first few weeks he'll be in our room in his bassinet Reece's parents bought. I look around the room and stop at the dresser. The picture of Reece and I is missing. I look in the top drawer and behind it, but it didn't fall either way. Maybe Reece took it and was planning on replacing it.

I turn off the light and head back downstairs. Reece is out messing with the grill. I see burgers on the counter, so I get some potatoes out and slice them up for homemade fries. Those are his favorite. He comes in and wraps his arms around me. "Homemade fries?"

"Yep. I thought I'd make your favorite side dish. I'm going to steam some broccoli too." He hates that I make him eat his vegetables, but I told him we needed to be good role models for the baby. Again, he pouted because our son won't be eating solid foods for a long time. "You like broccoli, so quit bitching."

After dinner I lie on the sofa with my feet in his lap and let him massage them for me. I swear his massages make me sound like I'm starring in my own porno. I situate myself so I'm kind of on my side, but with my feet still on him.

He's watching some show on Netflix, and my eyes feel heavy. I don't bother trying to fight it.

I wake up later as Reece gently shakes me. He helps me upstairs and I stagger into the bathroom to get ready for bed. Reece comes in and wraps his arms around me while I finish brushing my teeth. The smell of my toothpaste mixed with his manly, woodsy scent wrap around me. I quickly rinse and put my toothbrush away.

"Look how sexy you look." He holds my gaze in the mirror but I turn away, shaking my head. "No? You don't see what I do." His hands grab the hem of my nightgown and pull it up my body. First, exposing my thighs that are a little shapelier than they were pre-baby, and my belly comes into view next. I've been lucky and haven't gotten stretch marks on my belly, but there are some little ones on my hips.

"Look at that belly. You're growing our child in there." He pulls my nightgown the rest of the way off. "I'm not going to lie, but I fucking love your tits. They're fuller and more sensitive now."

To punctuate his statement, he drags his thumbs over my nipples, and I moan as he pinches them between his thumb and pointer finger. I feel the wetness between my legs, and my panties stick to my lips. I don't even get embarrassed at how wet I get for him anymore. It'll probably never stop being like that.

He presses his lips to my neck, still watching me watch him in the mirror. "Fucking gorgeous," he whispers as he holds one breast, and the other hand slips inside my panties. My head rests on his shoulder as he zeroes in on my clit.

I hold onto the cool marble counter with one hand and wrap my other arm around the back of his neck. My lips part, and a moan slips out. "Delilah, look at yourself." I do as he touches me. My skin is flushed looking, my eyes are bright, and my blonde hair is wild around my shoulders. "Pure fucking beauty."

Two fingers enter me and his thumb strokes my clit. I begin to come hard. My mouth opens in a wordless cry as my pussy clamps down on his fingers. I turn my mouth up to his, and our tongues tangle as I ride the aftershocks of my orgasm.

Reece pulls his fingers from me and brings them up to my mouth, and I suck them inside. I moan at the tangy, sweet taste of myself as he watches me in the mirror and I watch him back. "Fuck me, please," I whisper.

A growl rips from his throat, and next thing I know my panties are gone. His lips touch my ear. "Hold on, baby." I grab onto to the marble counter and tilt my hips back.

Before I have time to react, he thrusts inside me to the hilt, and I cry out. His grip tightens on my hips. I watch him as he watches me. This is the hottest thing I've ever experienced. The tingling low in my belly starts, and I know my orgasm is close. I reach between my legs and begin rubbing my clit.

"Are you going to come for me?" I nod. "Good. Take yourself there." I do and in seconds I begin to come, and then he follows behind me. The hot splash of his cum inside of me triggers aftershocks that make me moan and grind against him until he's leaning over my back and we're both breathing heavy.

Reece kisses my sweaty neck and whispers quietly, "Marry me?"

Tears leak from my eyes, and every fiber of my being wants me to say yes—no, to *scream* it—but I don't say anything. I open my mouth, and then close it.

I whimper as he pulls his softening cock from me. He turns me around and tips my chin up. "You'll say yes when you're ready."

I wrap my arms around him and hug him as tight as I can. "Thank you." I hope he can feel how much that simple question meant to me.

SECURITY BREACH

After a few minutes he helps me put my nightgown back on, takes me to bed, and then follows me in, and with my belly pressed against his I fall asleep in his arms.

***

"Babe, my mom just pulled into the driveway," Reece hollers up to me. Elizabeth is taking me for a pre-baby spa day. She wants me nice and relaxed when the baby comes, which could be any time now. At least according to my OB, because I'm already dilated to a three and my belly has dropped.

Anxiety has consumed me and the thought of pushing out Reece's giant son out of my vagina has me freaking out. Every time I share this with him he laughs at me, and if I could get my leg that high I'd kick him in his balls. I secure the end of my braid with a rubber band and grab my lavender duster. I'd found a larger size at the store of the one I wore the night I met Reece…the night our son was conceived.

As a matter of fact, I'm wearing an outfit almost identical to that one. Instead of boots, I'm wearing my ballet flats, and my t-shirt and black leggings are maternity ones. I waddle as fast as I can down the stairs and feel like my child is trying to jam his head out of me.

Sex has also become borderline painful, so Reece has just had to get blowjobs, but he doesn't seem to mind. For me usually he gets me off with his hand or his mouth. Speaking of my man, he meets me at the bottom of the stairs. He smiles at me as he looks me up and down. Does he remember?

"You were wearing the exact same outfit when we met."

I stop in front of him. "You remember?"

"Of course baby, I remember everything from that night."

Elizabeth interrupts us when she knocks and comes in the front door. "Hey guys. Oh my gosh, Delilah, you're absolutely glowing." She stops in front of me. "How are you feeling? Are you ready to get pampered?"

"Uh…hello. Are you going to acknowledge your son?" I turn and look at Reece, rolling my eyes. He winks at me before going to his mom to give her a kiss. "Have fun, and keep an eye on my girl today."

"She's going to be in good hands."

I grab my purse and my phone and then Reece walks us out. At the passenger door, I look up at Reece and smile. "Who's babysitting me today?" He cocks an eyebrow. "You know who my dad is. I know someone is always tailing me. I'm not dumb."

Reece shakes his head. "It's Dalton."

I love Dalton. He's one of the funniest guys I've ever met. He reminds me of the lean, buff version of John Krasinski from *The Office*. His beard even looks like the actor's. The main difference is Dalton is British and used to be part of the SAS—the Special Air Service. He, like most of the other guys, is "a pussy magnet," as he likes to call himself, and a bona fide badass.

"Kiss her so we can go," his mom calls from the open window.

SECURITY BREACH

He bends down and kisses my lips. "Have fun. I'm meeting some of the guys at your dad's to play cards. If I'm not home when you're done, just text me."

"No, hang out with the guys. I feel like I've kept you from doing stuff with them."

"Babe, I'm a grown man and do what I want. I love spending time with you." He kisses my lips chastely and helps me inside. Then he stands in the driveway as we pull out.

"Thank you," Elizabeth says from the driver's seat.

"Thank you? For what?" I ask.

She smiles as we drive down the street. "Thank you for making my son happy. I'm sorry I ever doubted you two."

I grab her hand and give it a squeeze. "I only want to make him as happy as he makes me. He's going to be such a great dad."

We pull into the parking lot of Serenity Spa and head inside. Elizabeth gives them our names. A woman with dark-brown hair that's pulled back in a sleek ponytail comes toward me. "Ms. Mackenzie, I'm Raven, and I'll be doing your prenatal treatments today. If you'll follow me, we'll get you into one of our luxurious cotton robes, and then we'll go over the menu so we can decide what treatments you would like."

Elizabeth gives me a smile and thumbs-up before I'm led to the back. Raven shows me to a little room to change out of my clothes, and I moan when I put the extremely soft robe on. I slip my feet into the little slippers they left for me. A soft knock sounds at the door, and Raven pops her head in. "Follow me." We head down the hall and get started.

I've been buffed, polished, and massaged. I feel relaxed, but energized—it's weird, but it feels good. At one point during my facial I fell asleep and was totally embarrassed, but she assured me that it happens a lot.

She has me sit in this little room that looks like a café after I get dressed. Windows along the side offer me a beautiful view. Lake Michigan can be seen in the distance, and the sun rays are dancing over the water.

I'm waiting for Elizabeth and then we'll eat a little lunch before leaving. The scent of coffee beans hits me and I would *kill* for a cup right now.

A man with reddish-brown hair comes to my little table with a cup. "What's this?" I ask.

He gives me a charming grin. "It's herbal tea. It's a special prenatal blend."

I thank him and then take a sip of the warm beverage. Whatever is in the tea tastes like citrus, but it's got a weird aftertaste. There isn't a whole lot in the cup, and I've already finished it. I pull my phone out of the pocket of my duster and send a quick text to Reece.

Delilah: Hey you. I feel so good, and so relaxed. I'm ready for this baby to come anytime now.

I watch the black dots dance and rub my eyes. Are they going in and out of focus? Am I *that* tired?

Reece: That's great babe. I'm taking all of your dad's money.

Delilah: Yay!

I stick my phone back in my pocket, and when I look up, the room looks like it's swaying. Wait, *swaying*? I close my eyes and take a deep breath, but when I open my eyes everything looks like it's going out of focus.

My heart tries to race, but it's like it's slowing down. Something's wrong, and I realize something was in my tea. Scanning the room, I find the man who brought it. "Wha you do?" My words are slurred. I've got to get to the front of the building. Grabbing the sides of the table, I try to hoist myself up, but it feels like my body is full of lead.

The man approaches me and I try to shrink away, but it's like I can't move. He lifts me with ease and I lie limp in his arms. "Your mom's waiting for you," is the last thing I hear as I fade into nothingness.

Chapter Nineteen

Reece

"Asshole, quit taking my money." Marcus pushes away from table and throws his cards down. He looks at Jack. "I'm out. Don't let Reece take all of *your* money."

We all laugh, and he gets up to grab a bottle of water out of the fridge. He sits on the sofa in front of the flat-screen while Jack deals the next hand.

Jack wanted us all to get together, especially since almost everyone is wrapped up with whatever case they're working on. He hasn't given up trying to find the guy who attacked Del, but he's got an old buddy that I don't know looking into things. All I know is it's an old Army guy who operates outside of the law and doesn't mind doing illegal shit to get things done.

After our next hand, my phone buzzes. Pulling it out of my pocket, I smile when I see it's a text from my girl. My smile widens as I read her words. She's been miserable the last couple of weeks while trying

SECURITY BREACH

to hide it and be strong, but my girl is losing steam. I was thrilled when my mom said she was going to come up and take her for a spa day. I'm sure they're having a good time.

My phone rings and I see it's my mom. I get up from the table. "Hey Mo—"

"H-He t-t-took her," she chokes out.

The hair on the back of my neck stands up. "What? Who took her?" I feel the men who've become my brothers standing behind me.

"S-She was waiting for me. S-Some m-man took her. I chased after them, but I tripped, and twisted my ankle." Her sobs come through the line. "I'm s-so sorry."

"Mom, it's okay. Did you call the police?" I don't have to look to know that the guys are following me to the door.

"Someone at the spa did. Reece, tell me what to do to fix this. D-Don't hate me."

I stop moving. "Mom, I don't hate you—I could never hate you. You could've hurt yourself running after them. I'm on my way to the spa now. We're going to find her, okay? We'll be there as soon as we can."

Jack steps in front of me. "Dalton just called—he was on their tail, but didn't want to spook him with Del in the car. They're on I-90 right now. We're going to find her."

I lose it. "How the *fuck* can you be *calm*? That's your fucking daughter! He's got my *life* in that car."

He grabs me by the front of the shirt, catching me off guard. My back slams into the wall, and then Erik is behind Jack trying to pull him off. Jack leans in close. "I'll let that fucking slide because you love my daughter, but you know as well as I do that we can't find her if we lose our shit." He slams me into the wall again. "Don't you *dare* act like I don't fucking care, because that girl is *everything* to me."

Our eyes stay locked, but Jack's phone rings, bringing us out of our stare down. He brings his phone to his ear. "Mackenzie." A pause, and I don't miss the way his jaw clenches. "Anyone hurt? Okay. I'm grabbing my laptop now. I have a tracker on her phone." Another pause. "I'll call you back.

Egan's already on his laptop. "Jack, I've got the app up and they're still heading west on I-90. You guys go; I'm going to see if I can hack into the spa's security footage to get a clear picture of him. I'll run his face through my software, and maybe if I can get a lock on who he is, it'll be easier to find out where he might take her." Egan looks at Jack, and then me. "We're going to get her back."

By the time we reach the spa cops are there, and my mom is sitting in the back of the ambulance getting her ankle wrapped. While Jack talks to the police, I make my way toward her. She throws herself in my arms. "She was in his arms, and she wasn't moving. Dalton saw me run after them. He stopped to make sure I was okay before he took off after them. She's getting so close to the end."

That's all I can think about. What if she goes into labor and the guy doesn't help her? She could die, our son could die—but no, that's not going to fucking happen.

We head north on I-90. Silence fills the inside of Erik's Explorer. I stare unseeing out the passenger window.

Jack's phone rings and he answers it, putting it on speakerphone. "What do you have for us, Egan?"

"I'm picking her phone up just outside of Crystal Lake. It's possible they dumped it, but it'll hopefully give us a good area to start searching. I've got his photos running through my system, and hopefully I'll get a match."

Egan texts us the coordinates for Delilah's phone's signal, and sure enough it's in the dumpster next to a Shell station outside of Crystal Lake. We pull over outside of the RV park and hop out as Dalton pulls up with Marcus behind him.

Dalton looks beat down. "Bloody hell that accident he caused was brutal." His British accent is a lot thicker right now. "Fuck me, I tried to get past it, but I fucking lost them."

"You're no use to us dead. You did what you could," I tell him and pat him on the back twice before we all gather around the hood of his car with Jack's tablet. He pulls up maps and starts going over search areas.

We're splitting up into three groups. Our plan is to check out as many places as we can before dark. Hopefully Egan will get a match soon, and then we may have a better chance at finding them.

Erik, Jack, and I are together, and we head toward the lake, looking for any signs that he took her into the woods. The bad part is that there are a lot of woods to check. It'll also be getting dark soon, and it'll be harder to track them.

"Remember he's driving a newer model blue Toyota Camry," Jack announces, and a thought hits me.

My stomach rolls as I remember finding a blue car in our driveway the day her mom showed up. "Jack?" He looks at me. "Becky showed up in a blue Camry, but I didn't pay much attention to it."

He shakes his head. "Becky is a lot of things, but she wouldn't hurt her daughter." Jack looks like he doesn't believe his own words. "She wouldn't."

I step toward him. "Think about it, Jack. That woman has been on her to get rid of our baby. The blows Del took to her stomach could've caused her to have a miscarriage. Everything that's happened has been centered on the baby."

Jack narrows his eyes and pulls out his phone again. After dialing a number, he puts it on speakerphone.

Becky's nonchalant voice fills the air. "Well hello, Jack," she purrs. "What can I do for you?"

"What have you done with my daughter?" he barks.

We can hear her clapping sarcastically. "I wondered how long it would take for you to figure it out. Color me impressed."

Blood rushes in my ears, and Jack's jaw is clenched so tight I'm surprised we can't hear his teeth crack.

"I suppose you have Reece there with you. Reece, we could've had fun," she says in a singsong voice.

"Bitch, I'd rather stick my dick through a barbwire fence," I spit. Jack gives me warning look. I turn away, trying to get myself under control. Her laugh through the phone sounds maniacal. A queasy feeling sits in my gut. "Where's Delilah?"

"Don't worry about her. By the time you boys find us, she'll already have spit that kid out, and he'll be gone."

"What the fuck do you mean? If you hurt my son or Delilah, I'll make you pay for the rest of your fucking life," I growl.

Erik steps in front of me with his hands on my shoulders and mouths, "Get it together. He's sent a signal to Egan to trace the call. We need to keep her on the line." I nod…reluctantly.

"Becky, please don't hurt our daughter. Don't hurt my grandson. You don't have to be involved if—Becky? Fuck, she hung up." Jack pushes some buttons and holds the phone up to his ear. "Did you get it?" He listens and then grunts into the phone. "Okay, we'll work with what we've got." Again, he stops to listen. "No, it's okay. This at least helps enough." He hangs up, looking at the two of us. "Let's go hunting."

Chapter Twenty

Delilah

When I open my eyes I groan, but it sounds muffled. I go to wipe my mouth, but that's when I realize I can't move my hand. My heart begins to gallop in my chest. I look around and see that I'm on a bed with my hands tied down and off to the side.

There's what appears to be an IV coming out of my hand. Looking down at myself, I see I'm in a nightgown. Straps are around my thighs, keeping my legs spread, and straps around my ankles keep my legs in place. My nose burns due to the dusty-smelling air.

I take a deep breath, trying to calm my racing heart. It can't be good for me or the baby if my pulse is racing. I try to move my legs, but they only move a little. I'm leaned against a mountain of pillows, thankful I'm not lying flat. My eyes go to the IV in my hand, and I follow the clear tube that runs up to a clear bag.

SECURITY BREACH

I see the word "Pitocin" on it just as my stomach starts to cramp hard. Moaning around my gag, it hits me what that is for. At the birthing class, they said that Pitocin was what they use for inducing labor. "No…" I moan around the gag.

I try to pull my arms loose, and then try to flip my hand over so I can work the needle out of my hand, but it's no use—I can't. Tears threaten to spill over when I hear gravel crunching outside, and I try one more time to get loose, but I can't.

The door opens and the man from the spa walks in, followed by…I begin to cry when I realize it's my mom.

She comes toward me, stopping on the side of my bed. "Hi honey. Are you comfortable?" I shake my head. "What do you need?" I turn away from her and find the missing picture of Reece and me, facing me from the little end table.

I tell her to let me go, but it comes out garbled. She sits down next to my hip and smiles at me, like I'm not tied to a bed. "I can't do that, but don't worry—I'm going to take good care of you. This is for the best, okay? The baby is going to a good home, and then you can go back to your life." She reaches out and plays with the end of my braid. "I know Reece made promises to you, but he'll break them just like your dad did."

My stomach tightens and I moan, trying to curl in on myself. "Mom, please stop this," I say around my gag as tears leak from my eyes.

The guy that came in with her comes over to the IV and fiddles with the machine. "Delilah, your contractions might start getting a little stronger." He looks at my mom. "We'll check her in a little bit and see if she's dilating."

My mom looks at me. "He's a medic. Don't worry, he knows what he's doing."

I turn my face away from her. Why couldn't she just leave me alone? I never wanted to see her again, and now she's trying to take my baby. She gets up, and the guy follows her out of the room. I wiggle around, trying to get loose, but they've got me strapped in tight.

I've got to have faith that Reece and my dad will find me. In the other room, I hear moaning before the sound of flesh slapping. My stomach turns violently as my mother's moans drift through the very thin walls. She did that when I was younger too. Her men would come over and fuck her while I sat and watched TV, but hearing them the whole time.

My stomach tightens, and it's more painful this time. I moan, my body twisting on the bed. I take some deep breaths, trying to focus on anything other than the pain. When the pain fades, I relax into the pillows and start to cry.

The sound of my mother having an orgasm bounces off the walls, followed by the grunts of the man fucking her.

I'm unsure how much time passes before my mom comes waltzing back in acting like everything's cool. The guy follows her in and he grabs some gloves and a tube of something.

He stops at the end of the bed. "I need to check you and see if you've dilated more."

Check me, like he's going to put his *fingers* in

me? I fight against my bindings, screaming "no" at him.

"If you don't want to lose that baby, you'll let me make sure everything's moving like it should."

He sits down on the end of the bed, and I cry as I feel him put his fingers inside of me. It's not sexual or anything, but still this feels so wrong, and I just want to go home. After what feels like a long time, he pulls his fingers out and slips his gloves off before looking at my mom. "She's dilated to about five and a half. My guess is she's been in labor and hasn't really noticed it, or she's going to go really fast. We should be ready for that."

My mom sits down next to my stomach. "We're getting twenty-five grand for your baby. Isn't that great?"

Just when I think I can't hate her more, she does something that makes me loathe her so much I want to vomit. I turn my head away from her; I can't even look at her right now. I begin contracting again and try to curl in on myself. My mom places a cool washcloth on my forehead. As the pain fades, I pant around the gag.

That was closer to the last one. This can't happen here. I refuse to let them take my baby. I may *look* like my mom, but I'm my father's daughter. I need to get my mom to believe that I'm agreeable to their plan. Maybe then she'll untie me. I'm hit with the desire to pee. "Mom," I say around the gag. "Mom."

"Don't scream, okay?" she tells me, and I nod.

Once the gag is taken out of my mouth, I open and close my mouth, stretching my jaw. "I have to pee." I don't even care that her boyfriend or whatever is sitting right there.

"I'm not untying you. I've got a bed pan, and we could use that."

I shake my head. "I can't sit on a bed pan. Please just let me get up. Won't it be better to have me get up and walk around?"

"Fine, but I'm going with you." My mom and the medic undo my straps, and then they help me stand up. It takes a minute for the stiffness to loosen in my body. On the way to the bathroom, I begin contracting again. I hold onto the wall with one hand and cradle my belly with the other. I cry out, this one more painful. My mom turns to look at her friend. "They're getting closer together. Should you increase the Pitocin?"

"Next time I check her I'll see where we're at. Her contractions seem to be getting stronger." My mom follows me into the bathroom with the pole that has my IV attached to it. She doesn't even turn away when I lift my nightgown and sit down. After, I finish up and wash my hands the best I can with the IV in.

I look in the mirror and see that my mom isn't watching me. Looking around the bathroom, I try to find anything that looks like it could be a weapon, but my stomach sinks when I don't see anything. Another contraction hits me, having me grab onto the cold porcelain sink. My mom doesn't even try to comfort me through it—she just stands there watching me, looking bored.

When it ends, she does help me back to the bed. "Can I have a drink? Maybe some water?"

SECURITY BREACH

My mom nods and grabs me a glass of water. I drink down the cool beverage and sigh. I was so parched because I guzzle it down, not caring that it's running down my chin.

I set the glass on the table next to my bed. "Thank you." I try to keep my voice nice and calm, even though on the inside I'm trying to plan my escape. When I lie on the bed, my mom grabs the straps and then my arm. "Please don't tie me back up. I promise I'm not going anywhere." I don't want to plead, but for my son I will. "Please?"

"Becky, just let her be for now. She's not going anywhere for a while."

I look up at the man, and as I look closer at him, I realize he's the one who jumped me in front of my apartment. My stomach pitches, and I swallow the bile that climbs up my throat. My mom was behind that—she let that man hit me right in the stomach. My son could've died because of her. "It was you," I grind out.

The brown-haired man stares at me with a smirk on his lips. "Becky, I think she figured it out."

I look at my mom, and she doesn't even look remorseful. A contraction starts up again and I cry out, gripping my stomach. I look at him and grit out between clenched teeth, "You're so dead."

He jerks his hand out and grabs my hair, making me scream. He gets down right in my face. "You better watch what you say to me, darlin', because what your mom doesn't know is I've got a *real* nasty temper. I'd really hate to do something that could hurt you enough that I've got to cut that kid out of you." I moan and wrap my hands around my belly.

"Mitch?" I hear my mom say from beside me. "Stop, you're scaring her." She laughs like it's funny.

"Becky, shut the fuck up." He looks at his watch, and back at me. "It's time to check you again. Behave, because I can make this a *lot* more painful." I nod because I'm not stupid. I won't risk my child.

My mom helps me lie back, and I turn my head away. I stare at and focus on the picture of Reece and me as Mitch sticks his fingers inside of me. "Shit, you're going fast. She's about seven centimeters and almost completely thinned out."

"I had her really fast. From beginning to end it was about four hours." She strokes my hair. "It won't be long before we get that mistake out of you. You'll be able to have the life I was supposed to have, but instead I had you."

My insides shrivel up at her words. I was nothing more to her than a mistake. My baby was *not* a mistake, and I would never regret him. I'm going to shower him in so much love he'll never doubt that we wanted him. Why didn't she give me to my dad if I ruined her life?

My body is covered in a fine sheen of sweat. I'm so tired, but I don't dare fall asleep. I need to figure out how to get out of here. I push off the bed until I'm standing. My mom moves in next to me. "What are you doing? I need to tie you back up."

"Can I please walk around for a little bit?" I look between the two of them, trying to keep my voice calm. "Where am I going to go?"

SECURITY BREACH

"Fine, but stay in this room only," he says, and stomps out of the room.

I hear the front door open and slam shut. I start to have another contraction and hold onto the wall as the pain becomes too much. I cry because how am I supposed to get away when the contractions are closer together? My mom doesn't offer me any comfort or support while I contract. I just breathe through it, and imagine that Reece is whispering in my ear, telling me that I'm doing great, and soon our son will be here, and to just let my body do what it's supposed to.

Once it fades I start pacing back and forth, or as much as I can with the pump and tubing keeping me close. Mom gets up and I'm assuming it's to go find Mitch. The front door opens, and I hear his voice. I move away from the opening.

The sound of someone snorting pulls my attention to the other room, followed by my mom's giggle. I move toward the window, and slowly ease it open. Peeking out, I see that the drop is too far for me to go out it.

I shut it and pull the IV from my hand, ignoring the blood running down my hand because if I see it, I'm going to pass out. I poke my head out where my mom and Mitch disappeared. They're making out on the couch; I don't miss the mirror with white powder on it, or the bottle of wine.

I'm hoping now that the medicine is no longer pumping into my body that my contractions will slow down. I look around the room, but make sure I stay hidden so they can't see me. The door is near the sofa where they're presently making out. Could

I make a run for it and be out the door before they could stop me?

I head back into the room as I begin to have another contraction. I put my fist in my mouth, biting down to keep from crying out. I can taste blood, and I don't know if I broke the skin or it's from where I pulled the IV out. Again, I don't look—I can't. I pant through the pain; this time it lasts longer.

When it ends, I move into the bathroom. I look at myself in the mirror, and cringe. My blonde hair is still in a braid, but I've got pieces sticking out all over. My cheeks are flushed, and my eyes are bright. I place my hands on my belly. "I promise I'm going to get us out of here," I whisper.

I look around for a weapon of any sort. I'm not afraid to use violence. I'll die before they get their hands on me or my son. My eyes land on the toilet, and I realize I've got the perfect weapon. I grab the lid that sits on the tank.

I sit down on the toilet as I begin to contract again. This time I can't hold in the moan that rips from my lips. *Oh shit*, this is it. They're going to be coming. Once the contraction slows, I take a deep breath and stand up on wobbly legs. I clutch the cool porcelain in my hands.

Someone starts pounding on the door, and it makes me jump. "Open the fucking door," Mitch barks at me. "If I have to bust down this door, you're going to be sorry." The doorknob jiggles. "Open the door. I'm not fucking around." I hear him yell at my mom, "Come get this bitch to let me in!"

"Delilah, just open the door. We're not going to hurt you."

"You're not taking my son," I shout.

I can hear them arguing. Someone stomps off, and a door slams. Banging starts again along with another contraction, and I begin to moan and cry, leaning against the wall. Something slams into the door, and I know it's Mitch. This is my chance. I stand next to the door with the lid raised up.

This time when he slams into the door, it opens and I bring the lid down on his head, knocking him down. The lid breaks apart and I drop it. I move to step around him as a gush of water hits the floor between my legs. "Nooo…" I moan. Where's my mom?

I grab my belly as I feel more fluid run down my legs. I try to walk through the pain, and once it fades, I move on quick feet to the door. I don't see my mom anywhere, so I take off toward the road. I only make it about a hundred yards before I begin contracting again.

I lean against the trunk of a tree and cover my mouth with my hand, trying to muffle my screams. That doesn't work so I sink my teeth into my forearm. More fluid leaks from me, and I feel a pressure between my legs that I didn't feel before. As soon as it fades, I hold my belly and try to run.

"Delilah!" I hear my mother's voice, and I move toward the woods to use the trees as cover. "Get back here!"

I keep moving, ignoring the pain in my feet from the pebbles digging into my skin, or the fact that it's gotten chilly. I've got one objective, and that's to get as far away as I can from them. The sun is setting, casting a dark shadow in the woods, which is better for me to hide in.

My knees hit the ground as a contraction so strong hits me I cry out. I hear pounding footsteps and try crawling toward some brush to hide, but a hand grabs my hair. I look up into the very angry eyes of my mom. Before I can react, she slaps me across the face. "You're ruining everything."

Mitch comes stumbling into the clearing with blood running down his face. My eyes start to flutter shut, but he lunges at me and starts dragging me by my hair back in the direction we just came from. "No, let me go!" I shout, hoping someone hears me. Another contraction hits me, and I scream. The urge to push hits me hard, but I fight it. I can't do it out here—I can't do it around the people that want to take my baby.

My mom stands in the clearing, shaking her head at me. "Why do you have to be so difficult?"

"Mom," I moan. "Please don't d-do this." Mitch lets go of me and I fall to my side, clutching my belly. "I have to push." Mitch moves toward me, but I scramble away in a crab walk.

He puts his hands on my knees. I try to kick him away, but I begin contracting again. Mitch lifts the nightgown and looks at my mom. "I see the head. Go get some towels—we can't move her." He turns to look back at me. "If you would've just stayed where you were, I'd at least be able to give you something for the pain. Now you get to suffer."

"Fuck you," I scream in his face.

He raises his hand like he's going to hit me when

SECURITY BREACH

I hear a twig snap. "You touch her, and I won't hesitate blowing your fucking brains out."

I look behind me and find my dad, Reece, and Erik with their guns drawn on Mitch. Then like in a movie there's a flurry of activity, and what looks like the whole team shows up. Reece tackles Mitch before anyone can stop him, punching the asshole twice in the face before Erik pulls Reece off so he can bind Mitch's hands together with some zip ties.

Marcus has my mom with her hands zip tied in front of her and leads her over to where they sat Mitch.

Reece gets down next to me, smoothing my hair out of my face. "You're here," I say lamely.

He gives me that devastating grin of his, but when he opens his mouth to speak I cry out, clutching my belly. "I have to push, I have to."

My dad gets down in front of me. "Baby girl, let me have a look, okay?" He lifts the nightgown. "Someone give me their shirt, and I need something to tie the cord off." He looks at me, his eyes shining bright. "You're about to be a mom."

As soon as the contraction hits, he tells me to push. Reece gets behind me, and I rest my back against his chest. He reaches down, grabs my thighs, and pulls them back as a scream rips from my throat. There's an intense burning, and I feel like I'm being torn apart. They tell me to push again, and with all my might I push until I feel something slip from my body, and then the sweetest sound I've ever heard. My son's cries are strong and loud.

I look at my dad, who's looking down at the

baby and then back up at me. "Uh...I think the ultrasound was wrong." He holds my "son" up. That's when I notice there's one vital part missing. "It's a girl."

Reece kisses the side of my head and hugs me to his chest. Dad lays my daughter in my arms. She's covered in Erik's shirt, and I kiss her little cone head. My eyes drift to my mom, who isn't even looking at me or her grandchild. Hollowness fills me, and I look away. Thankfully I don't have time to dwell on it because the ambulance has arrived, and the paramedics are coming toward us.

Chapter Twenty-One

Reece

Delilah slept most of the way to the hospital once they delivered the placenta. Rage filled me when I saw the bruise blooming on her cheek, knowing that one of them put their hands on her. It took everything I had not to shoot either one of them on the spot. Now that asshole Mitch is sitting behind bars, along with Del's crazy mother, and they can't hurt her or my daughter anymore.

My daughter…my daughter is fucking gorgeous. When Jack held her up and said, "It's a girl," I felt warmth in my chest that I've never experienced before. The moment she was in Delilah's arms, it multiplied by a hundred.

She's perfect—ten fingers, ten toes, dark-brown hair on her head, and chubby cheeks to die for. Del's sleeping, so my girl and I have been bonding. "Are you daddy's pretty girl?"

She yawns and brings her little fist up to her mouth, and I smile down at her. A knock at the door has me turning. My mom and dad stand there with flowers and a blue teddy bear. I can't wait to tell them that he's really a *she*. "Hey guys, come on in. Del's sleeping." My mom looks at her as they walk in and gives a soft smile. "Would you like to meet your granddaughter?"

My mom holds out her arms, but then freezes. "Grand*daughter*?"

I smile. "Surprise! Apparently, the ultrasound was wrong, because *he* is really a *she*."

"Congratulations, son." Dad claps his hand on my shoulder. "What a beauty like her mother."

I hand the baby to my mom, who cradles her to her chest. "Oh my. She's a big girl, isn't she?" She smiles at the baby. "You are such a pretty girl." Mom rocks her slowly back and forth. "How's Delilah?"

"So far she's okay. She's been quiet, but I figure the adrenaline rush is wearing off."

"I still can't believe it was her mother. My heart breaks for her, having a mother like that. She was willing to sell your baby."

Rage fills me when I think about it, but I push it back. "She's in jail. My guess she won't be getting out for a long time."

They leave a short time later, wanting to give us a chance to rest. Everyone else said they'd come tomorrow, including Brandon. He'd been out of town for work for the past month, and I know he's desperate to see them, especially when I filled him in on what happened, but he agreed that both girls need their rest.

The baby begins to cry, and my guess is she's

SECURITY BREACH

hungry. I turn to Delilah and see she's watching us. "Hey, baby. I think our girl is hungry. Do you want to try nursing?" She nods, and I call the nurse.

"Hi guys, I'm Stella. What do you need?" The nurse, an older redhead, uses some foam stuff on her hands.

"We think the baby's hungry, and Delilah wants to try nursing."

"Okay, great. Delilah, I'm going to sit you up." The head of the bed rises. Stella sets a pillow in Delilah's lap. "Okay Dad, I'll take the baby."

I hate giving her up to a stranger, but I'm not leaving her side. She sets our daughter in Del's arms, and then pulls the front of Delilah's gown down, exposing her breast. Our daughter is a genius, and immediately latches on to that nipple. I sit on the bed next to Delilah and kiss the side of her head as we watch our daughter eat.

***

My mom helps Delilah get dressed in the bathroom after her shower. My girls are coming home today, and we still have to pick out our daughter's name. Every time I ask Delilah, she shrugs her shoulders and says she wants to think about it. I'm sure it's just because she's exhausted. Brandon showed up first thing in the morning with breakfast and held and doted on his goddaughter—so much so that I finally had to take her back.

When Egan and Carrie show up, Brandon pulls me into the hallway. "Is Delilah okay? She seems quiet—withdrawn." Her friend's clearly worried.

"Do you blame her? Her mom was going to steal her baby and sell it. To make matters worse, she had to deliver the baby in the woods."

"Fucking Becky...she's always made it her life mission to put Del down, to hurt her. Becky always thought having a girl that she was getting a partner in crime, a best friend, not a daughter. Del was not wild like Becky. She was always quiet, loved to read, and was always studious. Who teases and makes fun of their child for getting good grades? Moving here was so good for her, and when she got pregnant, she thought maybe her mom would be happy, and they'd bond."

"But that didn't happen," I say, and Brandon nods. "I'll keep an eye on her and stop by whenever you want to see them. It'll be good for her to be surrounded by people who love her."

Brandon steps in close. "Thank you for being a good guy. I worried about her when she got pregnant, wondering if the guy who did it was a total douche, but clearly she got very lucky. You're great, Reece." He claps me on the shoulder and then disappears down the hall.

Now, as I step back into the room after running home, I know I need to keep an eye on things. I find my mom braiding Delilah's hair, our daughter cradled in her arms. I give her a smile when I sit down across from them. "Have you thought of a name yet?" I ask her. "I like the name Charlotte." It was my grandmother's—my mom's mom—name. It's classic, but I love it for my princess.

"I like it." She turns to my mom. "What's your middle name?"

SECURITY BREACH

I'm curious as to why she asked that.

"It's Jane."

Delilah looks at me. "Charlotte Jane Meyers. That's her name."

I won't lie—I'm a little choked up right now, because it's perfect. My mom hugs Delilah from behind and kisses her cheek. "Thank you, beautiful girl."

I call the nurse in so they can register our daughter's name for her birth certificate and social security card. After that, I run down to get the car while Mom stays with Delilah. Once the valet brings my 4Runner up, a nurse is wheeling Delilah out with my mom following with Charlotte in her carrier.

I get both of my girls settled into the back, and my mom gets into my dad's car. They're going to stay with us for a couple of days to help, which I'm thankful for because my anxiety grows the closer we get to home.

I'm thankful we've been so busy since the baby came because I haven't had time to think about those few hours I didn't know where she was, or if she was okay. Turns out that piece of shit who took her was a paramedic and stole all the stuff they needed to deliver Charlotte. At least he knew what he was doing. When we came up on them, the shit head had his hand up and was ready to strike her.

Her screams while she'd pushed our daughter out had scared the shit out of me, but the moment my little girl cried, I'd wanted to do flips.

I pull into the driveway and tell Delilah to wait and I'll come help her out. After I do, my mom and dad, who pulled up next to us, grab the bags for me while I grab the carrier.

We get inside and I get the baby out of her carrier, passing her to Delilah so she can nurse her. Then I want Delilah to lie down and take a nap. She needs her rest. My mom follows them upstairs. I flop down on the sofa and tip my head back, staring at the ceiling.

"You okay, son? I know it's a little overwhelming at first, but you'll find your rhythm. That's why we're only staying a few days. Your mom's going to make some meals. All you'll have to do is pop them in the oven. We'll keep an eye on the princess so you guys can get some sleep too."

"Thanks, Dad. I'm glad they're both home, and safe. I'm just freaked a little, but I'll be okay."

"Your grandma would be so pleased that your daughter has her name. It was really sweet that Delilah gave her your mom's middle name as well." He sits down next to me. "We'll order out tonight, our treat. I'll call Jack and see if he wants to join us." I hug him quick.

I head upstairs and on silent feet I move toward the nursery, which I'm going to have to repaint. The sight in front of me makes me melt; Delilah is sitting in the rocker while the baby is to her breast. My mom's talking to Del quietly while stroking my daughter's head. I back away, giving her and my mom some private time, which I have no doubt my girl needs, and head to my bedroom to change out of my jeans and into a pair of basketball shorts.

When I'm walking back by the nursery, Delilah and my mom come walking out, my mom with

SECURITY BREACH

Charlotte in her arms. Delilah comes right to me, wrapping her arms around my waist. We head downstairs, and I get her all snuggled up in the corner of the sofa. In minutes Delilah is sound asleep.

Her dad shows up and we share dinner, letting Delilah sleep while Charlotte is passed around getting love from everyone.

***

"Good morning, Shayla," I say as I step out of the elevator.

She gives me a smile. "Good morning, Reece. How are Delilah and Charlotte?"

My baby girl is two weeks old today. We seem to have a pretty good routine down, but we know that could change at any time. Charlotte nurses for about a half hour, every three hours. Delilah's been doing well about not overdoing it, and sleeping when the baby does.

I can tell she's exhausted, but she doesn't complain at all. My baby girl is a pig, and she's twelve pounds. At her two-week checkup the day before, she was at the top of the growth chart. She got a shot, and I swear her little face turned purple before a scream left her little lips. It was traumatic, and I know she's too little to remember, but I will.

"They're great." I pull my phone out of my pocket and pull up the picture I took of Charlotte in her bouncy seat that Jack brought over last week.

She takes the phone. "Oh my goodness. She gets prettier and prettier every time I see her."

I take my phone back. "Thanks. She's starting to look like Delilah for sure."

"Tell her I'm going to come see her soon." I nod as I step through the doors to the back. Jack texted me earlier and asked me to come in. I set my bag down and go into the breakroom to grab a cup of coffee, and then head to Jack's door, knocking twice before opening it. He's on the phone but he signals for me to come in.

"Yeah, tell them we'll get the quote to them as soon as Egan can come out and look around." He pauses. "Great, thanks." Jack disconnects his call. "How'd Charlotte do after her shots?"

"Shit, she only got one, but you'd swear someone was murdering her. By the time we left *I* was ready to cry."

Jack smiles and leans back in his chair. He's quiet for a minute, and then his brow furrows. He sighs before shaking his head. "Okay, this isn't easy, but I think something is wrong with Delilah."

"What do you mean?" Have I missed something?

"Do you notice that when Del's holding the baby that she doesn't ever really *look* at her? She doesn't talk to her, or coo at her, either. If you have the baby, she avoids looking at you. It's like she's detached or something."

Shit, is she not bonding with our daughter? "I'll keep an eye on her, and let you know if I notice anything." Of course I try thinking back to whether I've noticed anything out of the ordinary. Granted we're both so exhausted, so maybe I've missed it.

When I get home later, Jack's words ring in my head. I come in through the garage and find Delilah curled up on the sofa watching TV, and the baby is in her bouncy seat. I'm not too suspicious of that because we can't hold her all of the time. "Hey baby." She gets up and comes toward me, wrapping her arms around my waist. I wrap my arms around her. "How was our girl today?"

She pulls away from me. "Fine." I follow her into the kitchen. "I'm making spaghetti and garlic bread for dinner. Is that okay?"

"That sounds great." I grab her hand and pull her toward me. "You okay?"

Delilah smiles up at me. "I'm great."

Maybe her dad was just imagining things.

Later, after Delilah nurses the baby, I give Charlotte a bath, and when I come back down after putting the baby to bed in the bassinet in our room, I find Delilah curled up fast asleep on the sofa. I leave her while I watch the news for a bit, and then lock up before carrying her upstairs. I try lying down, but my mind won't shut off. Instead of tossing and turning, I get up and go downstairs to watch TV some more.

The sound of crying pulls me from my sleep. I realize I'm on the sofa. I grab my phone and check the time. It's one in the morning. I shut the TV and the light off before heading up. When I reach our room, I realize it's not the baby I heard crying, but looking at our bed, it's empty. The sound is coming from the closet. I open the door, flip on the light, and find Delilah curled up in the corner.

"Del baby, what's wrong?" She doesn't answer—just continues to cry. "Baby, if you don't tell me what's wrong, I can't help you."

She looks up, and the look in her eyes scares me. "I have to l-leave. I-I c-can't be here."

"What are you talking about? Why do you have to leave?"

"I'm no good for you. I'm no good for her." She keeps repeating it over and over.

I reach out, brushing her tangled hair out of her face. The tears continue to fall as she looks at me. "No good? What makes you say that?"

"I can't be around her. I'm going to hurt her."

Grabbing Delilah by her shoulders, I look deep into her eyes. "Why? Why can't you? You can't make statements like that and not give me a reason." Her eyes are wide and panicked.

Her chin wobbles, and she tries to pull away, but I don't let her. "Let me go," she cries, but I don't. "Don't m-make me s-s-say it. I can't."

"Don't you love her?" She whimpers, and my heart breaks. I can see she does so much, but she won't let herself. "She loves you. *I* love you."

"I don't want to turn into my mom. She didn't w-want me, and every day she made sure I knew what I was, and that was a meal ticket after she divorced Dad. Nothing I did made her proud. I was too nerdy for her…she wanted a girlfriend, but I had to be the grown-up because she didn't want to be. She paraded man after man in front of me, they never did anything, but I didn't miss the looks, the lingering stares. I was miserable, and I don't want that for her."

"You are *not* her."

"My mom's mom had her young, and was terrible to her. My mom had me young and was terrible to me. She was supposed to be a boy, so I could break the cycle. I can't have a girl—I'm going to turn into my mom, and I can't do that to that beautiful little girl, I can't."

I'm such a fucking idiot. How could I not see that she's been struggling? "Come here, baby." She crawls into my lap, and I hug her to my chest—letting her get it all out.

When she finally stops crying, our little lady decides she's ready to party. "Let's get her fed, changed, and settled back into bed. Then I want you to let me hold you. Tomorrow I think we should talk, and maybe talk to your dad too." She nods her head against my neck.

I help her stand up, and she goes right to the bassinet, scooping Charlotte and hugging her to her chest. She sits on the bed with her pillow in her lap, and gets the baby latched onto her breast. Delilah strokes her finger down the baby's cheek. "I'm so sorry, baby girl. I just didn't want to hurt you."

I maneuver myself behind her and wrap my arms around her. I stroke her hair and kiss the side of her head while watching our daughter eat. She certainly doesn't mess around when it comes to her food.

When she finishes eating, I change her diaper and she goes right back to sleep. Then I go about doing what I told Delilah I'd do.

I hold her all night.

Chapter Twenty-Two

Delilah

"Have you thought about what I said during our last session?" I stop picking at my thumbnail and look up at Melissa, the therapist I've been seeing since shortly after the night Reece found me in the closet. I've been diagnosed with anxiety and mild depression. Most of it was brought on by the ordeal I went through, but also the extremely toxic relationship with my mom.

I opted not to use medication. Instead, I've cut meat out of my diet again, begun doing yoga, meditating, and using essential oils. Occasionally I write in a journal, but that's only when I have a bad day.

I hate that I've missed so much bonding with Charlie—what I love to call her—the first two weeks of her life. I've made it up to her, I hope, in these past few weeks. We have our morning chitchats while I have my one cup of fully loaded coffee. Then I wear her in a little sling while I pick up around the house. We usually take our morning nap together, and I get up before her so I can shower.

Reece has been coming home for lunch, usually joined by my dad, who is so smitten with his granddaughter, and I love it. I'm sure they come—yes, to see Charlie—but to check on me as well. They both wanted me to go on medication, but I wanted to try a more natural approach first, especially since I plan on nursing her as long as I can.

After they leave, Charlie eats, and then sits—or I should say, *sleeps*—in her bouncy seat while I do yoga, and then meditate. After that, we usually run errands if we need to.

Having a daily routine helps so much, and on the weekends, Reece sticks to it because it keeps me focused and in control. Sometimes I can even get him to do yoga with me, but usually he grabs me and we start making out.

We have about two more weeks before we can resume sexual activity. The other morning, I gave Reece a blowjob while he used his fingers on me until we both came. It wasn't the same, but for now it'll do.

I felt like after everything that's happened the last few weeks he deserved it for being so great. Of course his response was he was a guy, and they'd revoke his man card if he turned down a blowjob.

"Delilah?"

Melissa pulls me from my thoughts. "I'm sorry. I don't know if I'm ready to face her." My mom's tried to call me a few times, but I've refused to talk to her. "There's not much that I have to say to that woman."

"Your anger is understandable. She was going to take your baby and sell her. You suffered a lot of abuse at the hands of that woman." Melissa doesn't sugarcoat things. She says it how it is, and I appreciate that—as painful as it is sometimes to hear. "You're not her. The fact that you kept yourself from bonding with your daughter to protect her from who you thought you'd become says a lot. The fact that you're here says how much you love Charlotte."

"I just feel like a fool," I blurt out.

"What makes you feel like a fool?" She sets her notebook down.

"For believing that she loved me at all, for believing her when she came to visit, that she wanted to spend time with me, that she was excited about the baby coming...but no, she tried to get my boyfriend into bed, and claimed she was testing him. She was about two hundred feet from me when my daughter was born, and she didn't even look at me or the baby."

"Your mom deserves to know how she made you feel. Even if she ignores you the whole time, at least you'll have released that pain. Give that pain back to your mom."

By the time my appointment is up, I've decided that I'm going to go see my mom. She's at the Cook County women's correctional facility. I can say what I want to say, and then I never have to see her again.

I head home and pull into the driveway next to

my dad's truck. Reece is busy working a case, so my dad agreed to babysit. I step inside and smile at the sight in front of me. My dad is lying on his back on the sofa, and Charlie is asleep on her grandpa's chest. "Hi, baby girl," he says. "How was your session?"

I sit down on the floor next to the sofa. "It was good. I'm going to go see Mom. I'm going to tell her how I feel, and then I'm going to walk away." Dad looks at me, and I know what he's going to say, but I hold up my hand to stop him. "Don't say it, Dad. Neither of us is at fault for her behavior and the choices she made. Sure, I wish that my mother loved me, but I've got a dad who does. Reece loves me, and this little princess loves me, and that's all I need."

He sighs. "Okay. If you're sure that's what you want, then I'll support you, baby girl."

My dad leaves shortly after that. I nurse my girl, then we take a nap.

***

Reece pulls into the parking lot at Cook County Jail. I'm here to visit my mom for the one and only time, and I'm a nervous wreck. In my head I've rehearsed what I'm going to say to her, but now that the day is here, I'm clueless.

My leg bounces up and down, and Reece reaches over and places his hand on my thigh. "We don't have to go in." He'd said yes immediately when I asked him to come with me. "I can pull right out of this parking lot."

I undo my seatbelt, crawl across the arm rest, and right into his lap. I grab his face with both hands. "I'll go. Thank you so much for coming. Thank you for being so patient and sweet while I dealt with things. I love you, Reece. I love you so much that the thought of not spending the rest of my life with you makes me sick." I take a deep breath before kissing his lips hard. "Marry me," I whisper.

He doesn't say anything and I start to get nervous, but then his lips are back on mine. I immediately open to him, his tongue dancing with mine. I whimper as he slows the kiss, and then pulls away. His smile is sweet, and slightly cocky. "Are you going to be my wife?" His eyes drift to my hand, and that's when I realize he slipped a ring on my finger. It's a simple platinum band with a princess-cut diamond. "I've been carrying that in my pocket, waiting for the right time."

"It's beautiful." I grab his face and kiss him. "I can't believe I proposed in the parking lot right before I'm going in to see my hot mess mother in jail."

"Delilah, I don't care where it happens. I love you, I want you to be my wife, and when you walk in there, I want you to feel that ring on your finger, and know that I'll be right there with you, supporting you, loving you."

He hugs me tight, and then I get back in my seat, check my face in the mirror. We climb out, and I wrap my coat tighter around me. Reece wraps his arm around my shoulders, and we head inside. He's going to wait in the waiting room for me. I give him my coat and purse. I walk through security, sign in, and stick the visitor's badge on.

My palms sweat as I make my way to an empty table and wait. The smell of sweat, sadness, and something else fills the air, burning my nose. It takes about five minutes before I hear a clanking noise, and then I see her walking toward me. Of course she looks good—I shouldn't have expected anything less.

I don't bother standing up and keep my face expressionless. I don't want to let on that I'm nervous. She sits across from me and neither of us speaks. My hands rest on the top of the table, and I know my mom notices the ring, but doesn't say a word.

"Why did you want to see me?" I ask. This woman is taking time away from my daughter.

"I wanted to see how you were doing. How's the baby?" She stares at the table.

I'm honestly surprised she's asking because I know she doesn't care. "I'm going to be fine, and my daughter is amazing."

"*You're* going to be? What's *wrong* with you?"

Wow, she's pulling out her superb acting chops.

"Thanks to the trauma I endured, and your wonderful parenting, I'm being treated for anxiety and mild depression." Was that a flinch I saw? It doesn't matter. "I was so scared when they said the baby was a girl that I was going to become you, and ruin that little girl, that for two weeks I would barely look at her. I'd feed her, change her diaper, but I wouldn't bond with her at all. I know I'm not you because I actually care about hurting my daughter. You never cared if you were hurting me.

You never loved me." It hurts to even say it.

"Well for what it's worth, I'm sorry. I wasn't cut out for parenthood. Your dad talked me out of having an abortion, and when he wanted full custody I should've given it to him instead of threatening to take you away." She stands up. "Will you send me pictures of her? I'd just like to see her picture as she gets bigger. I know I don't have the right to ask, but that'd be awesome."

"I'll think about it." She nods before turning, walking to the guard, and disappearing through the door. Why was that so underwhelming? I don't know if I was expecting her to grovel and admit she did love me, but that didn't happen at all. It takes me a minute before I'm able to stand. When I do, I feel a lightness that I've never felt before.

When I make my way toward the waiting room, I feel myself walking a little taller. I push through the door and find Reece sitting in the uncomfortable plastic chairs. He stands as I walk toward him. I wrap my arms around his waist. My cheek rests against his chest. "How'd it go?" he whispers against my ear.

"It went as good as can be expected. I said what I had to, and I listened to her. She wants me to send her pictures of Charlie. I told her I'd think about it." I look up at Reece. "That's all I can do for now, think about it."

Hand in hand I walk out with my fiancé, and we head home to our daughter.

Epilogue

Reece

Two years later

The sound of laughter fills my ears when I step into the house. "Where are my girls?" I holler. I hear the pitter patter of little feet seconds before my daughter comes running toward me on her chubby little legs. Her light brown locks are in two curly pigtails on her head.

"Daddeeeee…" She launches at me and I hug her to my chest. I carry her toward the kitchen where I find my beautiful and very pregnant wife at the stove stirring something in the big pot.

"Hey baby." She tilts her head up and puckers her lips. I kiss her slowly and thoroughly until Charlie decides she's done being ignored and leans forward trying to kiss us both. "Oh, I'm sorry, princess."

She smiles at me with big brown eyes that are identical to her momma's. I set her down and she runs toward our brown Labradoodle, Jinx, that my parents bought for us for our 1st anniversary. They said Charlie needed a dog, and I'm glad they did because that dog is our girl's shadow. He's protective of her and hates when she cries. Of course I don't like it either. Delilah says I spoil her, but she's just as bad. I think about fifty percent of the time she lets our daughter sleep with us.

I just miss being able to fuck my wife when I want. I told her this next one was *not* going to sleep with us, no matter what. This baby is a boy, and we are ninety-nine percent certain that he is a boy. Of course I'll believe it when I see it.

"How are you feeling?" I wrap my arms around my wife's swollen belly.

"Good…tired. Our daughter could tell I was beat today—she was actually really good. Her papa picked her up today for lunch." Jack is the biggest pushover for our daughter. She just has to bat her eyelashes, and he does her bidding. "Go shower, and dinner will be ready in about fifteen minutes." She smiles up at me.

I stroke her cheek. "I can finish up if you want?" This woman gets more and more beautiful, and when she's swollen with my child, she's stunning.

"No, go shower. You stink." She pinches her nose, and I tickle her sides until she lets go of her nose.

"Tinky," I hear Charlie say from where she's lying on the kitchen floor. She pinches her nose just like her mom.

I point at her. "No, *you're* stinky. Pee phew." She giggles her little girl giggles and buries her little head under the dog's front paws. Delilah just shakes her head.

Upstairs I shower, and then throw on some flannel pants and a t-shirt. On top of our dresser a picture frame grabs my attention. It's from the night we got married, when Charlotte was six months old.

We got married at a little church, surrounded by our friends and family. Delilah looked like an angel in the antique white dress that skimmed over her curves and hit the floor with a little train. The sleeves were long and hung off her shoulders. It was sexy, and classic. Charlie wore a dress the same color that was adorable.

I wore a black suit, with a white dress shirt and no tie. The picture was taken at our reception. Delilah had her arms around my waist, Charlie was in my arms, and we're smiling at each other. I couldn't tell you what happened, but I know that all I felt at that moment was pure bliss.

Heading back down the stairs, the walls are lined with pictures of our girl, a family photo I did under protest, and one that Delilah and my sister arranged with all of us that we gave to our mom. The woman cried so we obviously did well…very well.

"Uh oh," I hear Charlie announce. She usually says that when she spills something or takes her pullup off and pees on the floor. *Lord, give me strength to get through potty training.*

I step into the kitchen. "Charlie girl, what did you—uh oh."

That's when I realize she's pointing at Delilah. I don't miss the puddle between her legs. "Well, I think you better call my dad."

With Charlotte, Del had been given a medication to bring on labor, and she went really fast. This time we don't want to take a chance since they said the second baby can sometimes come quicker than the first. Jack sold his place in the city and bought a house ten minutes from us earlier this year.

I run upstairs and grab the hospital bag before changing into jeans and throwing some tennis shoes on. Delilah and Charlie come upstairs, and I help her change into some dry clothes. By the time we're heading downstairs, Jack is here.

He slaps me on the back before crouching down on the floor. "Come here, baby girl." Of course our daughter runs right to her papa.

He walks us out, hugging his daughter before I load her into the 4Runner.

Four hours later, our son Jackson Reece Meyers is born.

***

Delilah

One year later

I climb out of the SUV and make my way to the elevator. Carrie greets me, but when she sees my face, her smile dies. She pushes the button to open the sliding doors for me. In the back I can hear the men in the conference room. I stomp my way down the hall and find *him* sitting at the end of the table with Erik. He smiles when he sees me, but then he sees my face, it falls.

"What's wrong, babe? What happened at the doctor?"

"You refused to take your sample in after your vasectomy—well guess what, bucko? It didn't work, and I'm pregnant. Congratulations."

I'm not really mad, just in shock. We were happy with two healthy kids, and one of each. I told him over and over that he needed to take it in—that I would give him a blowjob to finish the job, but nooooo…he wasn't carrying around his cum. Sure he didn't mind asking *me* to take it in.

He comes toward me with a sheepish grin on his face. "Don't be mad. It's a baby—*our* baby."

I shake my head and smile up at him. "I'm not mad. Shocked, not mad, but I swear, if you don't get your vasectomy redone, or whatever it's called, we're *never* having sex again." I grab his face and pull him down for a kiss. "I love you."

"I love you too." He places his hand on my lower stomach. Ugh, this man knows how to make me melt, and I'm forgetting that I was ever irritated with him.

I poke my head in my office, and Shayla is behind my desk. She's the backup to Carrie and me when we're off, but she also helps with filing and anything else that is needed. She's become a great friend, and a great asset to the company.

"Hey Del, what are you doing here?"

"I had to talk to Reece. I just wanted to see if you got my notes about the order that was coming in."

She nods. "Yep, everything was good to go."

"Great. I'm heading to get the kids, but lunch tomorrow?" We're so busy now that we have to schedule our lunch dates.

"You got it."

I tell her goodbye and tell Carrie I'll call her later. On my way home, thoughts consume me. It's almost my mom's birthday, and although I haven't been back to see her, I send her a yearly letter with some photos of Charlie, and now Jackson. She's serving five years in prison for the kidnapping and attempting to steal my daughter and sell her.

With the help of my therapist, I've let go of the anger that was poisoning me and have even forgiven her. She'll never be a part of our lives, though—I just can't do it. She always sends me a generic thank you card and has sent Charlotte a couple of cards for her birthday, which surprised me, but she always signs them, "Becky." Not "grandma" or "Nana," which is what Charlie calls Reece's mom.

My dad made it very clear to her that when she's released that she's not to come anywhere near us unless that is what I want, and honestly, I don't know if that *is* what I want, ever.

I pull into the driveway and see that my dad is here, which is odd because our neighbor, Harley, is watching the kids for me because he was busy.

She moved in a year ago and has become a good friend. She's single, and gorgeous, and she won't let me set her up on any dates. Instead, she hangs out with us quite a bit and watches the kids for us. What I love that others don't know about her is that she writes erotic romance novels under the pen name Eva Steele. How cool is that?

I make my way inside, and Jackson comes

crawling to me. He turns one in a week and does not want to walk. He does this spider man crawl that's hilarious. If he has something he wants to carry, he'll put it in his mouth like a dog. He looks just like his daddy, and has the same bossy demeanor. "Hi, my monkey man." I scoop him up, covering his face in kisses.

I find Harley picking up toys in the living room with Charlie helping, and my dad can't take his eyes off her…hmmm, interesting.

"Hey, guys."

Harley gives me a nervous smile. "Hey, Del. How'd it go?" She knows that I'm pregnant, but only because she was there when I threw up.

I look at my dad. "I'm pregnant."

He gets up and pulls me into a hug. "That's great, honey."

"Yeah, this one was not planned at all. I'm super happy, but this is it. Three kids are perfect. What are you doing here?"

His eyes drift to Harley, and back to me. "I was just in the neighborhood, and thought I'd pop on by."

I'll let it go for now, but it makes me curious as hell about what was happening before I walked in.

Harley leaves right after that, and I promise her we'll talk later. Dad then leaves right after that. I'd mention something to Reece, but he'd tell me to stay out of it. What can I say—I love playing matchmaker, and I caught the matchmaking bug from Carrie.

I lay both kids down for their nap and sit down to write my mom.

Mom,

First, happy birthday, and I hope you're doing well. Things are well here. Both kids are doing great, and getting bigger every day. Charlie is so smart. She can count to ten and knows her ABC's. She loves her baby brother, but not so much right now since he loves getting into her toys.

Jinx just goes with the flow and does whatever the kids want. What can I say...they're spoiled ☺ I got the birthday card for Jackson; thank you for that. I'll keep it in a folder for him so he can see them when he's older.

I'm pregnant again, and it wasn't planned, but I'm still excited, but this will be the last baby. The two we have already keep us on our toes, so I can only imagine what another one will be like, but Reece is so great, and such a great helper.

Brandon and Jose got married this past summer, I couldn't remember if I told you. Charlie was their flower girl and loved it—she twirled down the aisle so much she *fell down spilling her rose petals, but she hopped right back up, and ran down the aisle to her daddy.*

I think that's all I have for now. I've enclosed pictures of the kids with the dog, and one of us from Brandon's wedding.

Take care of yourself...Please.
Love,
Delilah

I fold the letter around the photos I'll send her. Usually after I send her letter I need a drink, but obviously I can't have one now. Instead, I decide to lie down until the kids wake up.

***

Reece eases his softening cock out of me, and a whimper slips past my lips. He still makes my toes curl even three years later. I don't know what I was expecting—maybe for the sex to die down, or not be so toe curling, but if anything, it's better than ever.

He pulls me to him so we're chest to chest. "You make me so happy."

"Ditto, baby." I kiss his lips. "I never thought I'd find happiness like this. You've given me so much, and I don't know if I'll ever be able to thank you." Ugh, now I'm crying.

Reece kisses each tear away. "You've given me

an amazing family, baby. You love us so much, and that's all I could ask for. I should be thanking *you*."

Who knew that a one-night stand would turn into a love I could never imagine, and that I would forever be grateful for.

Eight months later, we'd be blessed again with the birth of our second son, Brandon Joseph.

The End!

Sneak Peek

STAKE OUT

Rogue Security and Investigation Series Book Two

Coming Spring/Early Summer 2018!

SNEAK PEEK

Shayla

I grab my coffee when they call my name at the counter and make my way to one of the chairs in the corner. I take a sip and sigh happily as the hot liquid slides down my throat. My coffeemaker broke this morning; the cat threw up in my doorway, which I didn't know until I stepped in it. While I hobbled into the bathroom, Grant—or as I like to call him, Grunt—came running past me, hit the throw up, and went sliding across my hardwood floor.

He immediately started crying. I grabbed him instead of cleaning my foot, so I could stick him in the shower and clean him up. Once he was dried off, I wrapped him in a towel and sent him to his room to wait for me. I quickly rinsed my foot before cleaning up the floor in my room. If I didn't love that cat so much, I might strangle him.

Once that was done, I headed into my son's room and leaned against the doorframe, watching him. He was lying on his bed looking at one of his picture books. Sadness washed over me when I thought about everything that'd happened over the past two years. My once fun-loving, joyful son is now quiet and overly sensitive.

My ex, Grant's father, used to hit me…bad, and I stayed because I was scared to leave because I had my child to think about and he loved his daddy. He loved him until he walked in on his dad pinning me to the bed, hitting and biting me until I was covered in blood and bruises. Ryan knew our son was in the room, but he didn't stop.

Grant was only three when it happened, and it was like someone had flipped a switch inside of him. The next day I went into the police station, pressing charges against him, and then filed for divorce. It was the last straw.

We moved to Chicago last year, hoping that a change of scenery would do him good, but so far it hasn't. He sees a therapist, but there's no change.

I sat down on his bed, glancing at the book he was looking at, and smiled. The *Dog Man* series is his favorite. We love going to the library, and he'll go through each page. I read with him, and work with him even though he doesn't talk. I'm hoping one day he'll snap out of it. Every day I'm hopeful.

My neighbor Luna watches him during the day while I work. She's a stay-at-home mom with three- and four-year-old girls. My sweet little Grunt does whatever they want, and they seem to talk for him so he doesn't have to.

He ran right over there when it was time to go. Grant always hugs Luna, and then both girls, but avoids her partner Rocco like the plague. I hate that he's so fearful of men, even the good ones.

"Shayla?" I'm pulled from my thoughts and look up to find my new friend Carrie coming toward me

STAKE OUT

with her cute pregnant belly.

"Hi girlie, you look fantastic."

The beautiful blonde rubs her belly and smiles. "Thanks." She sits down in the other chair. We met a few weeks ago when there were no chairs free for her, and I was on the loveseat. I'd invited her to sit with me, and we ended up talking for a little while.

My life is my son, but it's nice to have adult conversation. Due to my son, and him being non-verbal right now, I work for a temp agency, going where I'm needed, but with the flexibility I sometimes need. Luckily in the divorce settlement I got Ryan's 401k, which leaves me comfortable enough right now that I can work part time if that's what Grant needs from me.

"Are you getting ready for the baby to come?" She's due any time now.

Carries takes a sip of her tea. "We are. The nursery is ready, I'm doing cloth diapers and I've got the service set up. My bag's packed, and I've got the baby's coming home outfit picked up."

"That's exciting." I haven't shared that I have a son because then I'd have to explain that he doesn't speak, and then they'd find out about Ryan, and I'd rather keep that stuff private—it's easier that way.

"So, I have a question, and a possible request." She looks hopeful. "Okay first, I know you said you work for a temp agency, but I was wondering what type of work you do?"

"I do secretarial work, and when I lived in Madison, Wisconsin, I was the manager of a law office." That's why I was able to nail Ryan to the wall when I filed for divorce. I could've stayed working there, but after they learned the truth about my home life, I just couldn't do it. I had to leave.

"That's perfect. Okay, so my husband and I work for a security and investigation company called Rogue. Well, I go on maternity leave soon, and our office manager is searching for my replacement. She's expecting too, so we want someone that could step in and fill either role. This is just perfect that we met each other. It was like fate. You should come work for us."

"I'm not sure if I'm cut out for that right now. I just have some stuff that I'm dealing with," I tell her.

"How about this: I'll email you, or Delilah will. We'll give you a rundown of the job, the hours, and the pay. If you decide you want it, we can talk more."

I give her my email and drink the rest of my coffee down. I'm ready to say goodbye to her, but she stays me with a hand on my arm. "I have one more thing. I know you're single, and I was wondering if you'd be opposed to being set up on a blind date."

"I don't know. I'm not really in a good place to date." What I really need is to have sex. Masturbating is all I've done since my divorce. It's less complicated than sharing my history with someone.

"Oh, please. I've got the perfect guy for you. His name is Erik, and he's so much fun. Don't take this the wrong way, but you seem like you could use some fun."

When *is* the last time I had fun? I know Luna and

STAKE OUT

Rocco would watch Grant. "If I do this, I'll pick a place, and he can meet me." That way if it's disastrous, I can make my escape. Shit, maybe I could get some decent sex out of it, and then I'd be good for another couple of years.

Against my better judgment, I nod my head. "Ugh…Okay, set it up."

Right in the middle of the coffee shop, she starts squealing and clapping her hands.

I have a feeling saying yes was a mistake.

ACKNOWLEDGMENTS

First off, I want to thank my family. Your unwavering support means more than you'll ever know. Jim, every time I need you to step up and handle things while I write, edit, or market, you do—gladly. My sweet boys: Thank you for being tolerant of me when I'm the Queen of Grouchiness.

To my PA, Diane: Thank you for dealing with my flightiness, and for being the stickler I need to get stuff done. Thank you for handling all of my groups, promo stuff, and anything else that I might need.

To Angela: What can I really say except I love your face, and thank you for always supporting me, emotionally and mentally, when I need it. Our nightly writing sessions are what I look forward to daily.

Sydnee, my editor extraordinaire: I always, ALWAYS look forward to reading your notes on my manuscript. Even if I botch a whole scene, you don't ever make me feel like an idiot—you encourage, and that's what I love. Plus, with this story, a lot of your comments had me laughing my butt off.

Thank you to my readers and bloggers for your never-ending support. You make it possible for me to do what I do. I LOVE YOU ALL!!

As always, thank you to Team Limitless/Crave, from cover designer to formatter and everyone else. Thank you for believing in my stories.

ABOUT THE AUTHOR

A Midwesterner and self-proclaimed nerd, Evan has been an avid reader most of her life, but five years ago got bit by the writing bug, and it quickly became her addiction, passion and therapy. When the voices in her head give it a rest, she can always be found with her e-reader in her hand. Some of her favorites include, Shayla Black, Jaci Burton, Madeline Sheehan and Jamie Mcguire. Evan finds a lot of her inspiration in music, so if you see her wearing her headphones you know she means business and is in the zone.

During the day Evan works for a large homecare agency and at night she's superwoman. She's a wife to Jim and a mom to Ethan and Evan, a cook, a tutor, a friend and a writer. How does she do it? She'll never tell.

Facebook:
https://www.facebook.com/pages/Evan-Grace/626268640762539

Twitter:
https://twitter.com/Evan76Grace

Website:
http://www.authorevangrace.com/

Goodreads:
https://www.goodreads.com/author/show/7788444.Evan_Grace

Made in the USA
Monee, IL
03 September 2021